The Horses of Dereenard

Patrick O'Sullivan lives in Callinafercy, near Milltown, Co. Kerry. Both his uncle and his great-uncle wrote poetry, and he himself began to write short stories while still in primary school. Having studied History and Ancient Classics at UCC, he taught part-time in a number of schools. A lover of nature, he enjoys long walks by the river with his Labradors, Sweep and Sooty. This is his third book for Wolfhound Press.

ALSO BY PATRICK O'SULLIVAN

A Girl and a Dolphin
(Wolfhound Press, 1994)

Elsie and the Seal Boy
(Wolfhound Press, 1996)

The Horses
of Dereenard

Patrick O'Sullivan

WOLFHOUND PRESS
Celebrating 25 Years

First published in 2000 by
Wolfhound Press Ltd
68 Mountjoy Square
Dublin 1, Ireland
Tel: (353-1) 874 0354
Fax: (353-1) 872 0207

The Arts Council
An Chomhairle Ealaíon

Wolfhound Press receives financial assistance from The Arts Council/An Chomhairle Ealaíon, Dublin, Ireland.

British Library Cataloguing in Publication Data
A catalogue record for this book is available from the British Library.

ISBN 0-86327-790-X

10 9 8 7 6 5 4 3 2 1

Cover Illustration and Design: Angela Clarke
Typesetting: Wolfhound Press
Printed in the UK by Cox & Wyman Ltd, Reading, Berks.

For all the past pupils
of Callinafercy National School

Chapter One

*R*ebecca Sullivan was looking forward to the summer. Her mother had hinted at a family holiday somewhere special....

But then, out of the blue, came the letter from America. Rebecca's mother, Marie, was speechless at first: her cousin Anne was getting married, and they were invited to the wedding!

The trouble was that the invitation made no mention of Rebecca. 'What about me? What am I going to do?' she protested.

But her mother scarcely heard. 'Imagine! Anne getting married after all these years. She's the last person I expected to see walking up the aisle,' she said with delight. 'I thought she sounded different on the phone. I'm so happy for her! Things haven't always been easy for her, taking care of her mother for so long.'

Rebecca liked Anne too; but why couldn't she have

waited till the autumn to get married? That would have made life so much easier.

'She mentioned Dean a few times, but I thought they were just friends. He's very keen on music, like herself,' Marie Sullivan went on. 'We've always been very close, Anne and I. Once she told me she thought of me as the sister she never had.'

That was when it occurred to her that Rebecca could go and stay with her aunt Hazel in Kerry.

'But won't Hazel be invited to the wedding too?' Rebecca suggested. She didn't want to go to Kerry, and she was hoping she'd found a way out.

'Oh, she'll be invited, all right, but of course she won't go,' her mother replied. 'She could never leave her sheep and her goats for so long; she'd think something would happen to them.'

While Marie Sullivan had a great many friends, Rebecca knew that Hazel did not. Anne rang more often from America than Hazel did from Kerry; and as far as Rebecca was concerned, that was enough to suggest that she herself would be less than welcome if she arrived on Hazel's doorstep, suitcase in hand. 'Leave it to me. I'll arrange everything,' her mother promised with a confident smile; but Rebecca still had misgivings.

When her father came home from work, he was very pleased to hear the good news from America — though Rebecca sensed that he, like Hazel, would prefer to stay at home and simply send Anne a gift and their very best wishes. However, he knew how fond Anne was of his wife and how much she would be looking forward to seeing her at the wedding, so he agreed with all the plans that were suggested to him.

'Kerry won't be so bad; and Hazel will be glad of the company, though she'd never admit it,' he said, in an effort to reassure Rebecca.

'I suppose I'll survive for a few weeks,' Rebecca replied. Now that the initial shock had worn off, she didn't want to spoil things for her mother; but her mother still hadn't made the all-important phone call to Kerry, and there was still the possibility that Hazel might simply refuse to have her.

Marie Sullivan decided to postpone the phone call until the next day; she said something about catching Hazel in the right mood. At last she lifted the receiver and dialled the number, Rebecca in the background observing her closely.

Her mother tried to sound familiar and chatty, but there was something strained in her voice. She and Hazel were sisters, but sometimes it seemed as if they had very little in common.

'Well, what did she say?' Rebecca asked when her mother replaced the receiver.

Her mother sighed. 'If you must know, she said it was well for me if I could swan off to America at the drop of a hat,' she replied. 'But she knows as well as I do, we haven't been anywhere in ages.'

'But what did she say about me?' Rebecca persisted.

'Oh, she was fine about that,' her mother replied dismissively. 'Just say nice things about the goats or the ducks and you'll be grand.'

'You make it sound as if she has photos of them hanging on the walls or something,' Rebecca laughed.

'I wouldn't put it past her,' her mother retorted, more seriously.

Arrangements were made. Rebecca would take the train to Killarney and the bus from there to Dereenard — there was just one bus every day during the summer, and the service was even more restricted in winter.

A week or so later, Rebecca stopped and looked about with interest as she made her way up an incline to the old two-storey farmhouse where Hazel lived. The townland of Dereenard was a place of hills and sheep and sparkling streams, and the sun was shining down so that everything seemed more beautiful still.

Rebecca savoured the scent of the honeysuckle in the hedgerows for a moment or two, but when she began to move on again she couldn't help feeling slightly ill at ease. It would be so awkward if Hazel made it plain that she wished Rebecca hadn't come at all....

A brown-and-white sheepdog came running towards her and began to leap about her with delight. Rebecca put down her canvas bag and stroked him, and his tail wagged more furiously still.

'All right, Jack, there's no need to lose the run of yourself,' Hazel said, coming to greet Rebecca too. Hazel was in her early thirties; her short brown hair, neatly groomed, added to the look of severity and strength suggested by the lines of her face and by her deep brown eyes.

'He's lovely,' Rebecca said enthusiastically.

'He's lovely, all right,' her aunt agreed, 'but it doesn't do to mollycoddle them too much. It spoils them and makes them useless for the sheep.' She led the way inside.

Rebecca looked about the living-room. She saw that, while the room had been modernised, it still had an old-world character — peppermint-green walls, prints of country scenes above the hearth, holy pictures, and an oak dresser laden with old delft.

'I expect you're sorry you couldn't go to the wedding with your mother and father,' Hazel said, as she set about making tea.

'I was a bit disappointed at first, but then I wasn't

too pushed,' Rebecca told her.

'I can't see what all the fuss is about,' Hazel replied. 'Why can't people just go away and get married and have a quiet life for themselves?' Rebecca wondered whether this was a way of saying that, if Anne had chosen just such a course, Hazel wouldn't have been lumbered with an unwelcome guest.

A few moments later, they sat at the table and had tea and sandwiches together.

'Are you still drawing and painting?' Hazel asked.

'Now and then,' Rebecca replied. 'I brought my sketch-pad with me.'

'I'm glad to hear it. It's a shame to have a talent and let it go to waste,' Hazel said. 'I was hopeless at art in school, and I used to envy the people who were good at it.'

'Did you ever think of doing anything else besides farming?' Rebecca asked. Her aunt seemed more relaxed, at least for the moment.

'Oh, I thought of a lot of things, but I was very good with my hands — practical stuff,' Hazel explained. 'And when your uncle Tom and then your mother pulled out, I was the only one left behind with my father.' Rebecca knew that her uncle was now a vet in Cork, while her mother had trained as a secretary.

'My father and I didn't see eye to eye at times, but when it came to the crunch, neither one of us would let anyone say a bad word against the other,' Hazel went on thoughtfully. 'He used to say I was as good as any man for mending things — speaking of which, I have to go into the village later, for a part for the tractor, if you'd like to come with me.'

'I'd love to,' Rebecca said.

After their meal, Hazel showed Rebecca upstairs to her bedroom. Rebecca looked about her with renewed delight. Again, the room had an old-fashioned feel to it, but the view from the window was magnificent, the holly trees that sprouted about the hills glistening bright in the sunshine.

'Is that a forestry over there?' Rebecca asked, looking into the middle distance.

'Yes. It isn't owned by the government — by Coillte, I mean — but by the Stauntons; they've been in the business for years,' Hazel explained.

'Coillte? That's the forestry service, isn't it?' Rebecca said, and her aunt nodded. Rebecca wondered if she were imagining things, but Hazel seemed agitated. Was there something about the forestry — or, more specifically, about the people who owned it — that she didn't like? Rebecca decided not to press her on the subject, at least for the moment.

When her aunt went downstairs, she began to unpack. Everything about the room and the house suggested neatness and order. Rebecca was sure she would get a lecture if she left stuff lying around; she would have to make an extra-special effort to be tidy. It wasn't one of her strongest points; her mother gave out to her about it now and then, but such scoldings generally came to nothing.

Maybe her father was right, though: maybe Kerry wouldn't be so bad after all.

Some time later, Rebecca sat in the passenger seat as she and Hazel drove along the winding country road towards the village. She was still fascinated by everything she saw, and she noticed again that the houses were few and far between.

'We're a bit too isolated, too remote for a lot of people's taste,' Hazel said when Rebecca mentioned it. 'That doesn't bother me and Jack, though — does it, Jack?' There was an unmistakable warmth in her voice; despite what she'd said about mollycoddling him, the companionship she shared with the sheepdog was palpable.

Rebecca glanced back at the dog — who had his head through one of the back windows, which had been rolled down specially for him — and smiled.

'But most people have cars these days,' she reminded her aunt.

'Oh, yes, of course they have,' Hazel agreed. 'But one look will tell you that most of the land isn't up to much, and running after sheep isn't everyone's idea of fun.'

'But what about tourists? You'd think this would be just the sort of place they'd go for,' Rebecca said.

'We're too far off the beaten track for the tourists — and if you ask me, it's just as well,' Hazel replied, confirming Rebecca's impression that her privacy meant a great deal to her. 'We don't want to become a playground for tourists and nothing more.' Suddenly her tone was intense and serious again.

Rebecca began to understand what her mother had meant when she spoke about Hazel's love for her sheep and her goats. It was more than just a love of the animals; it was a kind of passion for the land itself.

Rebecca admired the trees in the forestry, but she didn't mention them again, as her aunt hadn't been very keen on the subject before. Did Hazel dislike the forestry as much as she disliked the notion of tourists swarming the roads? wondered Rebecca. But why should she? After all, she had admitted that most of the land was very poor — and what better way to make use of some of it than to plant it with trees?

The village was small and neat, the traditional shop-fronts painted in strong bright colours, the square dominated by the spires of the churches that stood on either side of it. When they came to the garage at last, Rebecca was intrigued to find that it was also a black-smith's forge. She followed Hazel inside and looked about her with interest, the anvil and bellows catching her eye at once. Hazel introduced the garage owner as Con Corcoran, and he shook Rebecca's hand with pleasure.

'Do people round here still use horses?' Rebecca asked as Con, a friendly middle-aged man, rummaged to find the part that Hazel needed for her tractor.

'They do, or at least Sam Staunton does,' he replied with a smile.

'The man who owns the forestry?' Rebecca guessed, remembering that Hazel had mentioned the name when she herself had asked about the trees.

'Yes. Most forestry places are all high-tech these days, but Sam still clings to the old ways,' Con said. 'They use the horses for drawing logs, and Sam says there's no better way of doing the job, especially on hilly ground like we have here in Dereenard.'

'The Stauntons have been in the business for decades,' Hazel said, and Rebecca didn't hear any resentment in her voice. 'Sam's grandfather started up just after the First World War; there were hundreds of forestry horses working in Ireland in those days.'

Rebecca was more intrigued than ever. Like most people, she had always associated horses with ploughing and sowing; but in Dereenard some of them, at least, had been put to a different use.

'The horses would nearly talk to you,' Con said, with such enthusiasm that Rebecca liked him at once.

'You see, just as Sam's people were always in the forestry business, my father and grandfather served their time as local blacksmiths; so you could say that the two of us are keeping up an old tradition.'

'Yes, but for how much longer?' Hazel asked. Rebecca caught the concern in her words, but she didn't ask her to elaborate.

'The horses are so well-behaved they could do the job themselves,' Con went on. 'They work hard, but they're well taken care of, and when they come in here it's a pleasure to look after their shoes and the like.'

'Oh, I'd love to see them at work,' Rebecca said longingly.

'And who's stopping you? 'Tisn't as if the forestry workers or Sam himself would stand in your way,' he smiled, pleased with her interest.

Rebecca looked to Hazel for approval.

'You'll have plenty of time to see them tomorrow,' Hazel promised, and again she sounded as if she were on good terms with the Stauntons. Maybe, Rebecca thought, she herself had simply misunderstood earlier in the day.

'It's lovely to think they're still using horses, but you'd think machines would be faster, and cheaper too,' she said as they returned to the car.

'Of course they'd be faster, but there's more to life than making money,' Hazel retorted with sudden conviction. 'Making a quick buck may be all right for today, but we have to think of tomorrow too.' They got into the car and Hazel switched on the ignition. 'And, like Con says, the horses are earning a living, which gives them a kind of dignity. They don't have to just depend on people to keep them and maintain them.' Again Rebecca heard the passion in her voice.

'I think it's brilliant,' she said with enthusiasm, and

Hazel smiled. She didn't smile very often, but when she did, her features were softened and she seemed altogether less intimidating.

Rebecca was in a thoughtful mood as they drove home. She wondered why her mother hadn't mentioned the forestry horses. Maybe she thought the Stauntons no longer used them. After all, it had been ages since she'd been to Dereenard, and most of the time she had very little communication with her sister.

A huge silver car came speeding towards them along the narrow road, and Hazel slowed to let it pass. 'That man!' she said, as the other car sped by. Rebecca looked at her curiously. Was she just angry because the car was travelling so fast, or was there something about the driver she didn't like?

As soon as they were back at the house, Hazel set to work on mending the tractor. Rebecca could only marvel at her knowledge and skill.

'It's fairly old, but I hitch the trailer to it now and then when I want to take a few sheep to the mart or move them from one place to another,' Hazel explained. 'Your mother and Tom think I'm a fool for wanting to keep this place going; but I suppose there's a place in the world for all of us, even for fools like me.'

Rebecca made no reply. She stroked and patted Jack, who was lying on the ground a little distance from the tractor.

'He's another one you can take with you on your travels tomorrow,' Hazel said, after a pause. 'He's mad about the horses, and there's a short cut through the fields.'

Rebecca smiled as she thought of the friendship between Jack and the horses. Her first day in Dereenard, and already she was beginning to think that maybe Hazel wasn't as crusty as she sometimes pretended to be, though there were clearly things about which she felt very passionate.

'And you can make yourself useful if you like. How about feeding the hens and ducks for me?' Hazel said.

Rebecca did as she was asked, grinning again as she thought of her mother's prediction that Hazel would have family portraits of the ducks on the walls.

Chapter Two

*T*he next day, Rebecca and Jack set off through the fields together towards the forestry. Yellow flags grew here and there, in damp places; the sun shone down, and Rebecca's blue eyes sparkled with anticipation. She could hardly wait to see the horses.

In a little while she came to the edge of the forestry and found a pathway. The scent of the trees was woody and green. She saw at once that there was more than one type of tree, and this surprised her: she had been sure all the trees would be the same. She heard the sound of a chain-saw and made her way towards it, Jack running on before her.

A few moments later the sheepdog began to bark with sudden delight, and Rebecca smiled as she saw a horse standing patiently in the shadows. She hurried towards the horse and stroked him.

'He's handsome, isn't he?' she said to Jack, and he

barked with still greater exuberance. 'He's got such a lovely dark chestnut coat, and his shoulders are so broad and strong.'

The horse seemed pleased with her attention, though he snuffled in her hands now and then as if he was expecting some sort of titbit. 'Oh, I wish I'd brought him something,' Rebecca said regretfully.

'I see you've met Rafferty,' said another voice, a friendly voice.

'Rafferty? Is that his name?' Rebecca asked.

'Yes, that's it,' the newcomer told her. He was in his early thirties, his hair wavy and dark, his eyes dark too, his frame muscular and strong. Rebecca thought at first he might be one of Sam Staunton's sons, but he introduced himself as Laurence Connor.

'Sam owns the forestry, but he lets the handling of the horses to foresters like myself,' Laurence explained.

He fetched a bag of oats and draped it about the horse's head. 'Old Rafferty gets a bit peckish at this time of the morning,' he said with a smile. 'And you must be Hazel's niece?'

Rebecca looked at him curiously, wondering how he knew who she was — but then, news probably travelled very fast in a small place like Dereenard.

'Have you always worked in the forestry?' she asked, admiring the horse all the while.

'Yes, since I left school. I never thought about doing anything else,' Laurence replied. 'My uncle worked for Sam's father, and my cousin works over there in another part of the wood, so we've kept it in the family, you see.'

Rafferty munched the oats with delight, and Jack eyed him curiously. 'We can't leave you out in the cold, you poor man,' Laurence said, tossing Jack a biscuit from a packet he withdrew from a carrier bag.

'Has Rafferty been here a long time?' Rebecca asked.

'Yes, he's been here a good few years now, but he's still strong and fit,' Laurence told her. 'Sam bought him from a man named Rafferty at Puck Fair. That's how he got his name.'

'His mane is so much darker than the rest of him — it's fabulous!' Rebecca enthused. She had noticed at once how well-groomed it was. His harness, too, looked in mint condition.

'There's no use having an animal unless you're willing to look after it. That's something I learned from my uncle,' Laurence said, when she complimented him on the harness.

'Would it be all right if I stayed a little while and watched Rafferty at work?' she asked.

Laurence nodded. He lifted a log and laid it across the metal bar attached to Rafferty's harness. 'Off you go now, my man, and take your time,' he told the horse.

Rebecca and Jack walked beside Rafferty as he hauled the log towards the pile at the end of the path, from where it would eventually be taken by lorry to the sawmill in the village. Laurence said he would follow them in a moment. There was no need to guide Rafferty; he knew the way himself. Sunlight came gleaming through the branches high above and added a deeper sheen to Rafferty's coat.

'I thought I'd have nothing to do all day, but this is brilliant,' Rebecca said happily. 'And Rafferty, you're the best!'

Something occurred to her, and she fell silent again. It was nice, she thought, that the same families had been involved in the forestry for generations — not just the Stauntons who owned it, but also the Connors who worked as foresters, and the Corcorans who had always been the local blacksmiths. There was a feeling of family about it all; and the horses were part of the family too.... She heard the singing of the birds, and again the woody incense of the trees filled her nostrils.

Laurence told her about the trees when he caught up with her. 'We've got lots of larch here. Do you see how soft and bright and green the needles are?' Rebecca sensed that his love of horses was almost rivalled by his love of the trees themselves. 'And the branches — they arch and droop and look so graceful.'

'Yes, they're lovely,' Rebecca agreed, though her praise sounded like an understatement after Laurence's words.

'We've got some spruce, too, but I prefer the larch myself,' he said. 'Best of all, there are some fine old oak and beech trees scattered here and there. You should see the beech trees in autumn — their leaves seem to blaze in the sunlight. Sam won't allow anyone to cut them, of course. He calls them his treasures.'

'Treasures?' Rebecca echoed.

'Yes, and he's right, too, isn't he?' Laurence said. 'The trees have a language of their own. They could tell us so much, if only we stopped to listen.'

They came to the end of the pathway, and another man helped Laurence lift the log onto the pile.

'I'll have to bring my camera next time, and maybe even my sketch-pad,' Rebecca said, stroking Rafferty again.

'Oh, you're an artist, are you?' Laurence smiled.

'I wouldn't say that, but I give it a go now and then,' Rebecca said.

She walked back along the pathway with her new friends. The more she saw of Rafferty, the more she admired him. Hazel was right: the forestry horses did have a kind of dignity about them.

It was some time before she and Jack made their way home through the fields again. Rebecca was happier than ever that she hadn't been invited to the wedding.

When Rebecca returned to the farmhouse, however, she heard raised voices in the living-room. She stopped dead in her tracks as she approached the door. Maybe it was wrong to eavesdrop, but something tempted her to wait and listen.

'You promised you wouldn't sell out, Dan. You promised,' Hazel was saying. 'And if people can't keep their word, there's no hope for any of us.'

Rebecca glimpsed Hazel's visitor through the window; he was a middle-aged man who looked old beyond his years.

'Ah, things have gone against me this past while — and, sure, I never thought he'd offer me as much as he's offering now,' he said. 'Besides, I'd be just as well off taking things a bit easy, at my time of life.'

'You'd swear you were ninety,' Hazel snapped. 'It was bad enough when he bought Murphy's, but now he has your place as well....'

'Ah, things might be different if a man had a family or something,' Dan said, still trying desperately to appease Hazel's anger.

'Will you stop making excuses, Dan? You couldn't resist the money, and that's all there is to it.'

'But, sure, what does it matter, Hazel? There's still yourself and John Coakley, and neither of ye will sell.'

'Well, I won't sell, anyway, Dan. I don't know what anyone else will do any more,' Hazel replied. 'No wonder Mr Warner thinks he can always get his own way in the end.' She paced about the floor; her guest was looking more repentant still. 'Don't you see, Dan? He'll see your decision to sell as another victory,' she went on. 'Divide and conquer. That's his game.'

'He'd have to buy Sam Staunton's too — the forestry, I mean — and there's no danger of that,' Dan said.

'Isn't there? Maybe Sam would be tempted too, if the price was right.' Hazel eyed her guest intently. 'My father would turn in his grave if he thought all this place was to be turned into one big forestry. What we have now are people who care about the place — the Stauntons. What we'd have then would be a big business that wouldn't give a damn about anything except making a quick buck.'

'Ah, now, I don't think Maurice Warner is as bad as all that,' Dan objected. 'And if his crowd did come in, they'd give great employment.'

'Oh, it's "Maurice" now, is it, Dan?' Hazel jeered. 'And I suppose he plied you with drink down in the village before he got you to sign on the dotted line. Well, let me tell you, he's not going to impress me with his talk of employment. Warners Wood Group aren't into horses, you know — more your high-tech timber harvesters — so all they'd need would be a couple of drivers.'

'Well, I thought I'd better come and tell you my news before you heard it from someone else,' Dan said, turning away.

'It's not the sort of news I wanted to hear, Dan,' Hazel said, more calmly. 'The land around here mightn't be the best, but people have made some sort of living off it for generations. We can't just let a stranger come in and do what he likes with it.'

Dan scrambled awkwardly down the hill towards his car. Now Rebecca understood what Hazel had meant in the garage, when she had asked how much longer the forestry horses would have work to do. Some big company wanted to buy up the land so that they could turn the Stauntons' forestry business into a much bigger operation.

When Rebecca went inside, Hazel told her briefly what Dan had come to say. 'You can't depend on any-one — that's something I learned a long time ago,' she said, resentment rising in her voice.

'But you have to trust *someone*,' Rebecca ventured.

'No, you don't. They just let you down,' Hazel insisted. 'And if Maurice Warner has his way, we'll have nothing but fast-growing spruce trees that can be planted and harvested in double-quick time.'

'It would be such a shame if they replaced the horses with machines,' Rebecca said.

'Warners wouldn't think twice about it. They don't go in much for sentimentality,' Hazel retorted. 'It's a pity the Connors don't own land close to the wood. They've worked with the horses all their lives, and they'd never sell up.'

Later that afternoon, Rebecca and her aunt paid another visit to the village. Hazel said she wanted to be sure that Sam Staunton was still on her side.

Rebecca was fascinated by the old prints and photo-graphs that hung on the walls of Sam's little office, the clutter of papers and files stacked here and there. Sam's hair was grey, but his soft blue eyes brightened with pleasure when he spoke of the forestry and the horses.

'There's my grandfather, and that's my father as a boy,' he said, pointing to a photograph. 'It's a pity I don't have a son of my own to carry on the business.'

'It's a bigger pity your daughter wouldn't take an interest in it,' Hazel replied candidly.

'Ah, she's too settled in her ways; she'd never leave the city,' Sam said.

The noise of saws echoed from the mill nearby, but Rebecca scarcely heard it. It was wonderful, she thought, that an unbroken line of horses had worked in the forestry for so long.

'A lot of places are beginning to appreciate the value of the horse again,' Sam told her. 'They have them in countries like Norway and Sweden, and even here at home, Coillte are making use of them too. So, instead of being behind the times, maybe we're ahead of them here in Dereenard.'

'But the man with the machine gets the same rate of pay as the man with the horse, and the man with the machine can work much faster — isn't that the trouble?' Hazel said wearily.

'Yes, that's the trouble in most places. But I don't have to tell you, Hazel, we've always paid our horse-men above the going rate,' Sam replied. 'There's plenty of men who can drive a machine, but it's not every-one who can handle a horse.' Rebecca liked Sam. His enthusiasm for the horses was palpable.

'And in bad weather, the horse doesn't do half the damage a machine would do; he doesn't churn up the ground and turn it into muck,' Sam went on. 'So all your nice undergrowth keeps growing the same as ever.' He smiled at Rebecca, pleased with her interest. 'And the horse can travel places where no machine would think of travelling.'

He sat down behind his desk again and looked at Hazel. He knew this wasn't just a social call; so what was troubling her?

'I just wanted to be sure you haven't changed your mind about selling out to our friend Mr Warner,' Hazel said.

'You can put your mind at ease. I've no intention of selling out to anyone, especially to the likes of him,' Sam told her, and Rebecca couldn't resist a grin of pleasure. It was clear that her aunt still had allies after all.

'I'd be lying if I didn't tell you we're going through a rough patch at the minute,' Sam admitted. 'The rumour machine is working overtime, of course, and no doubt Warner is after hearing of our troubles; but we've had tough times before, and we always pulled through in the end.'

'It wouldn't surprise me if he was the cause of your troubles,' Hazel said. 'He's the ruthless type, you know. Wouldn't think twice about turning your customers against you.'

'Oh, he doesn't have to. Matt manages that all by himself,' Sam replied dryly.

When they returned to the car, Hazel explained to Rebecca that Matt was Sam's great-nephew. The two of them didn't always get on too well. There had been something about a dispute over money, an inheritance, between Matt's grandfather and Sam, years before. But then Matt had needed a job and Sam had needed a manager, so they had been forced to put their differences aside for the sake of the business.

'But what did Sam mean about Matt turning their customers against them?' Rebecca asked.

'Oh, it's just the way Matt is — brusque, impatient, rubs people up the wrong way,' Hazel replied.

They fell silent again. As they drove home, Rebecca could see that Hazel was still worried. Yes, Sam was still on her side; but his business was in trouble, and if Matt had his way things might suddenly change.

At that very moment Maurice Warner was sitting in his office in Tralee, a map of Dereenard open on the desk before him. He was tall and slim, his hair neatly groomed, his brown eyes shining with satisfaction. He lifted the telephone, dialled the head office of Warners Wood Group and was put through to his brother, Philip.

'Things are coming along quite nicely in Dereenard,' he began. 'First I went after Murphy's place. That was easy — Murphy wanted to get out anyway. But Dan Quigley took a little longer to take the bait.'

'Time is money, Maurice,' Philip reminded him. 'We don't want this thing to drag on forever, you know.'

'You don't have to tell me that. It's these country people — some of them can be very stubborn,' Maurice replied. 'It isn't as if we're not offering them good money. The offer I've made Quigley is well in line with the market price.'

'What about the old man's great-nephew, Matt Staunton? Have you started working on him?'

'I'm just getting to him. He's not too happy with his lot, it seems,' Maurice laughed, a hint of slyness in his voice. 'Everyone has his price, and a man who's discontent is usually much more amenable than he might otherwise be.' He took a drag of a cigarette, then replaced it in the ashtray. 'I called in to their office. You should've seen it — nothing but clutter and files, here, there and everywhere. Apparently that's the way it's always been, the way the old man likes it. It's about time they were dragged kicking and screaming into the twenty-first century.'

He blew a smoke ring and watched it drift lazily in the afternoon heat. 'And the first thing to go will be those horses. Talk about slow-coaches! One of our machines would cover as much ground in a day as a horse can cover in a month.'

'I'm sure you weren't exactly welcome when you called in,' Philip said.

'You can say that again. The old man told me again that he wasn't the least bit interested in anything I had to say,' Maurice replied. 'The great-nephew was the one I was really hoping to meet, but he wasn't around. Still, no matter — I'll catch up with him one day soon.'

'See that you do,' his brother told him.

When Maurice replaced the receiver, he smiled to himself again. Timber harvesters weren't nearly as romantic as horses; but then, he had never been the sentimental type. If old Sam and his cronies only knew it, he would be doing them a favour.

Chapter Three

*W*hen Rebecca and Jack went to visit the forestry the next afternoon, they met a horse coming towards them along the pathway. Rebecca thought at first it was Rafferty again, but then she noticed that this horse was lighter in colour and that there was a blaze of white on his forehead.

She patted him when he came near, and his tail swished with pleasure. Jack barked with the same gusto with which he'd greeted Rafferty. Rebecca glanced at the graceful larch trees on either side of the path, and marvelled again at the thought that the horses of Dereenard were still working quietly away in the bright green world of the forest.

'Laurence mentioned his cousin. I wonder if this is his cousin's horse,' she said to Jack.

She noticed, however, that while Rafferty accepted Jack's barking as a display of affection, it made the horse beside her slightly restless. 'I don't think he's very keen on your singing, Jack,' she said.

Jack seemed to understand; he began to whine softly, as if to say he was only trying to be friendly. 'Good boy, good boy,' Rebecca said reassuringly, patting him. 'He looks a bit younger than Rafferty. Maybe that's why he doesn't understand.'

A moment later, she caught sight of a scar on the horse's right flank. She looked at it curiously. The wound had healed completely; but what could have caused it? Maybe there had been some kind of accident.

A man was coming towards her. It wasn't Laurence; this man was about the same age as him, but he looked rougher and more unkempt.

'Luke — the name's Luke Moran, at your service, little lady,' he said, the sunlight glinting in his green eyes. 'Looks a picture, doesn't he? But as bad-tempered as a mule.'

Rebecca looked at him uncertainly. She didn't understand. Had she been wrong to assume that Laurence's cousin would have the same feeling for the horses as Laurence himself? But then, Con at the garage had said they were all treated well.

'Horses are like everything else; you have to show them who's boss if you want to get any good out of them,' Luke went on. 'If Sam Staunton had his way, though, he'd stuff them with oats and give them all their own way.'

'I met him yesterday. He seems very fond of them, all right,' Rebecca ventured.

'Aye, he is — and that's the cause of all the bother; that's the reason they're so contrary,' Luke told her. 'A man couldn't say boo to them but Sam would be down on him like a ton of bricks.'

'But they work hard, don't they?' Rebecca said. This

was only her second visit to the forestry, but she'd seen Rafferty in action and there had been no slouching there.

'Work hard?' Luke scoffed. 'They don't know the meaning of it. Do you see the way they're rigged out, girl? You'd swear they were being made ready for a show.'

'You'd think being well-groomed and well cared for would be good for them,' Rebecca argued.

'That's what Sam believes; but, sure, it only spoils them and makes them soft,' Luke insisted, with the authority of an expert. Rebecca didn't like him very much. Despite his untidy appearance, there was an unexpected arrogance about him, as if he thought he and he alone knew what was best for the horses.

'And how's your aunt getting on?' he asked, turning to a new subject. Just as Laurence had known who Rebecca was, Luke knew that she'd come to stay with Hazel.

'She's fine,' Rebecca said.

'And has she any notion of selling up?' Luke probed.

'Oh, I don't know anything about that,' Rebecca said vaguely.

Her answer didn't satisfy Luke. 'Wouldn't it be an ease to her if she did pull out? She spends all her time chasing them sheep of hers,' he suggested, as if Hazel's happiness was his first concern. 'And Maurice Warner has all manner of plans for the place.'

Rebecca made no reply, but again she thought this was strange talk from one of Sam's employees. First he criticised Sam for being too soft with the horses, and now he was saying how much better off they all would be if Warners were allowed to go ahead with their plans.

'For one thing, they'd have the sawmills booming in no time; they wouldn't be the ramshackle little set-up

they are now. And that would be good news for everyone in Dereenard,' he went on.

He would have said more, but at that moment they
were joined by Laurence.

'What are you doing here, Luke?' Laurence challenged,
the annoyance in his voice thinly disguised.

'Oh, just paying a visit to my old stomping-ground
and having a chat with the little lady here,' Luke said.

'I don't think Sam would like it if he heard you were
snooping around,' Laurence told him.

'And who says I'm snooping around?' Luke countered,
with sudden resentment. 'We can't all be the teacher's
pet. I know full well that if you had your way, you'd
put up a sign saying, "Luke Moran: Keep Out"! But let
me tell you, you won't put me in my place that easily,
bucko.'

Rebecca hung on every word. The simmering hostility
between the two men was palpable.

'Look, Luke, I know you think the world and his
mother is against you, but you had your chance and
you didn't take it,' Laurence said. 'You were given a
good job here, but you blew it.'

'And why wouldn't I blow it, when you kept running
to Sam with tales?' Luke accused him. 'You had it in for
me from the first. You wanted the job for your cousin,
and you couldn't wait to get shut of me.'

Luke wasn't Laurence's cousin after all, Rebecca
realised, but he too had worked in the forestry for a time.

'Sam gave you plenty of warnings to look after your
horse, and he told you he'd send you packing if you
ever struck him with a stick again, but you thought he
was bluffing,' Laurence reminded him.

'Oh, it was all my fault, was it? Now why doesn't
that surprise me?' Luke jeered. 'You were working with
an experienced horse, Rafferty, but I was lumbered

with this fellow here — Star, if you please. He was some Star, all right, when it came to wanting his own way.'

'Star,' Rebecca repeated to herself. It was a lovely name, clearly inspired by the star-like blaze of white on the horse's forehead.

'I know he's a bit of a novice, but he's a quick learner, and he's picked up the tricks of the trade in no time at all,' Laurence told him. 'All he needed from you was a bit of patience and understanding.'

'Don't give me that old guff!' Luke snapped. 'The long and the short of it was that Sam wanted another member of the Connor clan, the famous horse-handlers, working for him; so I was given the high road, and your cousin got the job the minute he finished school.' He paused, and a smirk crept over his face. 'Oh, good old Sam loves talking about the old days, and having the Connors around keeps him happy; but take it from me, you and he are living in the past.'

Laurence sighed but said nothing. Luke turned and walked away.

'Nothing would give him greater satisfaction than to see Sam go under, having to sell out to Maurice Warner lock, stock and barrel,' Laurence said when Luke had gone out of sight, and again Rebecca heard the concern in his voice. 'He can say what he likes about Star, but no one has to tell that horse what to do these days; he knows the ropes himself.'

Laurence returned to his work. He and Rafferty were happy to have Rebecca and Jack for company for a little while again.

'There's a kind of music in the clanking of the horse's harness, isn't there? It's the loveliest sound in the world,' Laurence said. Rebecca nodded agreement. She wondered what he would do if there ever came a day when someone decided the horses were no longer needed in the woods of Dereenard. It was a prospect she didn't even want to consider; but what if it were to become a reality — sooner rather than later?

'Poor Star,' she said. 'I don't know how anyone, even Luke, could beat him with a stick.'

'Yes, it would make you wonder, wouldn't it?' Laurence agreed, smiling at her intensity.

Later that afternoon, Matt Staunton had some bad news for his great-uncle.

'Heffernans want to renege on our deal; they don't want us to supply them any more,' he said, his blue eyes shining with resentment. 'They know we're in a bit of a bind at the minute, so they think they can trample all over us.'

Sam rubbed his hand through his wavy grey hair; he had never felt so frustrated in his life. 'Are you sure you didn't say anything to upset them?' he asked.

'No, of course I didn't. What do you take me for?' Matt snapped. 'I crawled like a toady, like you told me to, but Helen Heffernan said she could get the stuff cheaper elsewhere, so we'd have to lower our prices if we still wanted to do business with her.'

The tick of the old wall clock beat time in the stillness, the pendulum swinging relentlessly back and forth.

'She knows our prices are as competitive as the next,' Sam said, rising from his place behind the desk and going to the window.

'Maybe Warners are putting the squeeze on them,' Matt suggested brusquely.

'That's a possibility — of course it is — but I don't think she was very keen on what you said about women in business when she came to see us last month,' Sam reminded him. 'And she was dead right. You had no business shooting your mouth off like that.'

'She got on my nerves,' Matt countered tersely. 'Our standard stuff wasn't good enough for her. She wanted special stuff of her own, even though she knew it would mean a load of hassle.'

Sam turned from the window to face his great-nephew. 'That's what business is all about — or didn't they teach you anything at that fancy college?' he challenged him. 'The golden rule is that the customer is always right, and we have to do our best to look after him — or her.'

'Looking after them is one thing, but pandering to Helen Heffernan and her ilk is quite another,' Matt retorted. If there was one thing he disliked more than anything else in the world, it was being lectured by the old man. 'Oh, I could see what she thought of me: a little jumped-up office boy, fresh out of college, with notions beyond my place.'

'So you thought you'd give her the benefit of your college education,' Sam snapped. 'Let me remind you of something, in case you've forgotten: the Heffernans have always been very good customers of ours, and Helen Heffernan turned that company around single-handedly.'

'The bottom line is, she wants us to drop our prices or she'll find another supplier,' Matt reminded him. 'So I told her we just couldn't agree to do it, and that's that as far as I'm concerned.'

'Oh, that's that, is it?' Sam said. 'Well now, do you know what you can do, Matt? You can take up that phone again, ring her back and tell her you've had second thoughts; maybe we can do something about our prices after all.'

'No. No, I won't. I've done enough crawling for one day,' Matt snapped. 'Besides, you said yourself our prices are as fair as she's likely to get anywhere.'

'I know all that, but it's a buyer's market, and if you hadn't put your foot in your mouth when she came to see us, she mightn't be making things so tough for us now.'

Matt dropped some invoices on the desk and eyed his great-uncle coldly. 'Look, it was you who appointed me as Manager here. You couldn't handle it all yourself, you said, and you wanted to give me a chance. But, just like today, every time I make a decision you have something to say about it.'

'Of course I have something to say about it! You waltz in and tell me we're about to lose one of our best customers, and you expect me to sit back and relax and take it all in my stride?' Sam asked. He sighed and glanced through some of the invoices for a moment. 'Look, Matt boy, this is a family business; we all muck in together and we don't get hung up on titles. That's the way it was in my father's time, and that's the way —'

Matt didn't let him finish. 'I don't care how it was in your father's time,' he snapped dismissively. 'I'm not going to ring that Heffernan woman again, and there's nothing you can say that will make me change my mind.' He stormed out of the office and slammed the door behind him.

Sam sat behind the desk and looked at the photographs on the facing wall. The trouble with Matt, he thought, was that he took everything personally. He was young and inexperienced and bound to make mistakes; but the question was, how long could Sam put up with his tantrums?

Later that evening, Hazel sent Jack off to round up the sheep so that she could dose them against disease. The sheep had to be dosed every now and then, she told Rebecca, as they watched Jack at work.

Rebecca marvelled at the sheepdog's skill and speed; it was as if he knew every inch of the hilly terrain by heart. Hazel whistled to him now and then, but he knew instinctively what to do, and while there was an urgency about him, there was also a certain restraint. When he came close to the sheep, he hung back a little, so that he brought them under his control without frightening or scattering them.

'He's marvellous,' Rebecca said with enthusiasm.

'He knows his job, all right,' Hazel agreed, a quiet pride in her voice. 'He has some very good breeding in him; he comes from a long line of dogs that were famous for their even temperaments.'

It struck Rebecca again that Hazel was never happier than when she was working about the farm, tending to her fowls or mending the tractor or looking after her sheep. She was more relaxed, too, now that she knew that Sam Staunton was still determined to resist all Maurice Warner's attempts to buy him out; and she had every reason to hope that her neighbours, the Coakleys, would be equally firm.

Rebecca watched with delight as Jack herded the sheep down the hill into a corral behind the farmhouse. Hazel clambered over the fence and set to work, giving each sheep a dose of medicine by a kind of spray into its mouth. It was strange to see the sheep all crowded into one place, Rebecca thought, their restless noises echoing through the sunlit stillness.

'I suppose they don't like the taste of it,' she said.

'No, I suppose they don't,' Hazel replied, her tone good-humoured, 'but then, it's like a whole lot of things that are good for you — it's fairly revolting stuff.' Rebecca saw that Hazel was very confident in her handling of the sheep: one hand gripped the sheep's neck firmly, the other inserted the nozzle into its mouth, and the dose was administered in double-quick time.

Soon they were joined by Laurence, who had finished work for the day.

'You should've waited for me,' he said to Hazel.

'I said I'd be making a start. Besides, you're tired after your day's work,' Hazel replied.

'Well, now I'm here I'll take over for a bit,' he said. Hazel handed him the dosing equipment.

'She's a great woman, but she's not very good at letting people help her out. Wants to do everything herself,' Laurence told Rebecca, when Hazel had gone inside to answer the telephone.

'It's very nice of you to help her,' Rebecca said. She sensed that Laurence had strong feelings for her aunt, if only she'd allow him to show them.

'Oh, now, she's good herself. She did a lot of good turns for Dan Quigley. That was why she felt so let down when she heard he was pulling out,' Laurence explained. 'And our friend Mr Warner is still on the prowl. He doesn't seem to leave the place these days.'

'Sam won't sell, and neither will the Coakleys,' Rebecca said.

'Oh, Sam won't sell — that much is certain; but I wouldn't put my money on John Coakley sticking to his guns,' Laurence told her. Again Rebecca was filled with unease. If the Coakleys sold their land to Warners, then Hazel's only ally would be Sam, and her farm would be the only one outside Warners's control — Sam just owned the forestry.

She was just about to ask Laurence what reason he

had for making these gloomy predictions when Hazel reappeared, and Rebecca thought it best to say no more. Hazel was in a happy mood, and Rebecca didn't want to throw a spanner in the works. Instead they talked about the sheep again. Laurence praised their healthy condition, which Rebecca regarded as an indirect compliment to Hazel — Laurence didn't have to be told how proud Hazel was of her flock.

When the work was done, Jack herded the flock back to the hills. They washed and cleaned themselves up, and Hazel insisted that Laurence should stay and have supper with them. Laurence was startled; this was something she had never done before. Maybe it was Rebecca's presence that made the difference, he thought. Rebecca helped to set the table, and in a little while they sat down to eat.

During a lull in the conversation, Rebecca thought of her mother and the wedding in America. She'd almost forgotten: today was the day her mother's cousin was getting married.

'They're all probably in the chapel now; they're five hours behind us, aren't they? Anne must be very excited and nervous and stuff,' she said.

'I wish you wouldn't keep talking about this bloody wedding,' Hazel snapped, with a sudden change of mood.

Rebecca, who had scarcely mentioned the wedding since her arrival, looked at her awkwardly. She sensed that Laurence was embarrassed too, but he said nothing.

'I'm sorry. I didn't mean any harm,' she said.

'Of course you didn't,' Laurence agreed. 'What I'd like to know is when you're going to get out your sketch-pad and draw me a picture of Rafferty.'

'I'll give it a go whenever you like,' Rebecca promised. She could see that he was tactfully trying to change the subject, and she liked him for that.

But when she went up to her bedroom, some time later, she wondered why Hazel had become so moody and disgruntled all of a sudden. She had spoken as if Rebecca had harped on about the wedding, morning, noon and night; and Rebecca couldn't see what was so wrong in mentioning Anne's big day.

Could it be that Hazel was jealous of Anne? Maybe at a subconscious level she resented Anne's marriage; maybe it made her feel more isolated and lonely than ever. After all, Hazel and Anne were often mentioned in the same breath — by Rebecca's mother, at least, who thought nothing of making comparisons and pointing out similarities in their lives; but now all that would change. Anne would be married, and Hazel would still be alone.

Rebecca lay flat on her bed and stared at the ceiling, deep in thought. One thing was certain: she couldn't take Hazel's moods for granted again.

Chapter Four

'*F*ind the weak link and go for it.' That had always
been Maurice Warner's policy in his dealings
with rivals and opponents of any kind. Young Matt
was the weak link at the Stauntons'; but what about
John Coakley? What was his Achilles heel?

Maurice was driving along the road in his big silver
car when he came upon Luke Moran hitching a lift.
Normally he didn't give lifts to anyone, especially not
to people like Luke; but at times like this, every scrap
of information could prove useful.

When the car slowed to a stop, Luke opened the
door and peered at the driver.

'Mr Warner, is it?' he asked, his green eyes shining
roguishly, a sly expression on his face.

'The very same. Can I give you a lift somewhere?'
Maurice replied.

A few moments later, they were driving along, Luke

sitting in the passenger seat. Maurice wondered how he could introduce the subject of most interest to him at that particular moment — namely, John Coakley — but it wasn't long before Luke began to talk of the forestry and Sam's management of it.

'He's way behind the times, and he can't even see it,' Luke said scornfully. 'Sure, anyone could see them horses are more trouble than they're worth, what with feed and vet's bills and blacksmiths.'

'I suppose it's the way he's always done things,' Maurice replied, not wanting to appear too critical — at least, not at first. 'Besides, machines are costly to keep going, too.'

'Ah, his operation is too small, far too small,' Luke persisted, with the authority of an expert. 'It's no wonder they're losing business; they just can't compete any more.'

'They've done well enough up to now, haven't they?' Maurice said. Until he was sure of Luke's motives and loyalties, he would create the impression that he was interested in fair play at all costs.

'I suppose they have, if you call barely ticking over "doing well enough",' Luke replied. 'But they can't keep going as they are forever.'

'Well, it's no secret that my company would like to take them over and expand the business,' Maurice said. 'I haven't been driving around Dereenard this past while just to admire the scenery, you know.'

'I know you haven't,' Luke smirked, his expression sly again. 'Isn't that why you're after buying up two farms? And I hear tell you're after more land.'

'Well, it's no good doing things by halves — that's always been our motto,' Maurice replied. Sunlight flashed on the windscreen, and he was tempted to grope in the glove compartment and put on his sunglasses.

'Some of the natives aren't too keen on selling, though.'

He slowed, lit a cigarette and offered one to Luke.

'John Coakley is after doing more to improve his place than the rest of them put together,' Luke said, taking a drag of the cigarette. 'Hired diggers and dug drains and built new outhouses. Them hayfields of his — sure, they were no better than bogs and rushes a few years back.'

'An enterprising man,' Maurice replied. 'He seems to be one of the few people who keeps cattle as well as sheep. I expect that's why he needs the hay.'

'You don't miss much, Mr Warner, if you don't mind me saying so. But I suppose you'll tell me you don't know the first thing about farming,' Luke grinned.

His companion smiled, but made no reply.

'All them diggers cost money, though, and Coakley had to borrow from the bank. They say he still owes them a fair bit.'

'Does he, now?' Maurice asked. He was intrigued.

'And that's not all. His missus is a townie, born and bred,' Luke went on. 'They lived in Killarney for a year or two after they got married, and John used be back and forth to the farm. Sure, he'd spend the day here, he hated the town that much.'

'And then they came to live in Dereenard?' Maurice prompted.

'Aye, they did; but though that's a good fifteen years ago, the little lady still doesn't like the place,' Luke said. 'She used to go out to work in Killarney, in a hotel or something, and now that her children are getting old enough to fend for themselves, she'd like to go back to work again. There's nothing for her here in Dereenard, and she says it wouldn't be worth her while driving in and out; most of her money would go on petrol.'

'That's interesting,' Maurice mused.

'Oh, sure, I'm an interesting man,' Luke said with a
smirk.

Rebecca spent the morning helping Hazel to mend
some fences; when someone kept sheep, Hazel told
her, mending fences was a neverending job. As Hazel
removed a post here and there and pounded replace-
ments into place with a sledgehammer, Rebecca was
impressed again by her aunt's skill and confidence.

Rebecca asked to have a go with the sledgehammer,
but she soon found she could hardly lift it. 'This thing
weighs a ton,' she said.

'If you came to Dereenard more often, we'd make a
fit woman of you,' Hazel replied. 'But I bet when your
mother told you that you were going to Kerry, you
never thought you'd be messing around with wire and
posts.'

'No, I didn't,' Rebecca admitted, 'but it's kind of fun.'

'Fun, she calls it — and my back ready to split in
two!' Hazel replied with a smile. Rebecca smiled too,
happy that her aunt's mood had improved again, at
least for the time being.

After lunch she found her sketch-pad and headed
off towards the forestry again. Laurence was pleased to
see her, and he watched with interest as she set to work
on a preliminary sketch of Rafferty.

'I'm not very good, and it takes me ages to get
things right, so don't be expecting a masterpiece,' she
warned him.

'You're like your aunt: you're too hard on yourself,'
Laurence said.

'Maybe I am,' Rebecca agreed. 'It's just that when I draw something, I like it to be the best it can be — but that's just with my drawing.' She grinned. 'You should see my room. If Hazel sees it, she'll freak out.'

'It's not that bad, is it?' Laurence asked, as he followed the movements of the pencil on the page.

'No, it's not that bad; but compared to the way Hazel keeps things, it's not very good either,' Rebecca told him.

Laurence returned to his work a moment or two later, and Rebecca sketched in silence for a while. Rafferty was taking a well-earned break, and it was almost as if he were posing for her, as if he liked the notion of having his picture drawn. Again she admired his heavy, powerful build and the marvellous gloss on his chestnut coat.

'When you've finished there, you can give me a hand to plant some of these saplings, if you like,' Laurence called out in a while.

'In a minute,' Rebecca called back. Laurence couldn't see her now, but her expression was intense and keen, every stroke of the pen patient and meticulous, as the outlines of the horse gradually began to take shape on the page.

When she closed her sketch-pad and put it aside, she went to help Laurence, marvelling at the beauty of the saplings — they were pot-grown, which meant they could be planted at any time of the year.

'We've mostly been thinning, this past while; but when we clear a patch, like we've done here, we restock it straight away,' Laurence explained. 'So if we take something out, we put something back too.'

Rebecca took a spade and began to dig a hole. She wasn't afraid to try her hand at things, and Laurence liked her for that.

'How's Hazel today?' he asked.

'Oh, she's fine,' Rebecca assured him.

Laurence packed earth around one of the saplings, then hesitated and looked at Rebecca. 'You know, when she snapped at you last night, when you mentioned the wedding — there was a reason for that,' he said.

'What reason?'

'Your mother didn't tell you?' Laurence asked.

Rebecca shook her head.

'Hazel was engaged to be married, a good few years ago now, but things didn't work out,' he told her.

'The man she was going to marry let her down or something?' Rebecca speculated, intrigued.

'No, no, it wasn't like that. In fact, if anything, it was the opposite,' Laurence replied. 'The arrangements were all made, the invitations all sent out; but at the last minute, Hazel decided that she couldn't go through with it, that she didn't really love him.'

'That must've been awful,' Rebecca said.

'Yes, it was. It would've been embarrassing for anyone, but particularly for someone like Hazel,' Laurence said. 'To make matters worse, her boyfriend was a very good sort; it wasn't as if she discovered some terrible flaw in him — as if he were a secret drinker or something. If she had, people might've been more understanding.'

'And people weren't understanding?' Rebecca asked.

'Oh, some people were all right; but you'll always get the few who make snide remarks. Hazel had too much of her own way, they said, and she'd never be satisfied if she wasn't satisfied with Joe,' Laurence explained. 'She didn't mind that so much, though; it was the thought of letting her father down that really seemed to get to her.'

'Her father might've been disappointed for her, but

why did she think she was letting him down?' Rebecca asked.

'Joe was a very good worker, very keen on making a go of the farm. He was going to move in with Hazel and her father, you see,' Laurence replied. 'Your uncle Tom was already working as a vet in Cork and had little or no interest in the place, so I suppose Hazel's father was keen on the notion of having someone like Joe to step into his shoes.'

'I wish I'd known. I wouldn't have even mentioned the wedding if I had,' Rebecca said remorsefully.

'Don't worry about it. Hazel's a tough customer; she doesn't take things to heart for long,' Laurence assured her. 'But now you see why she's so determined to hold on to her land. She blames herself for letting her father down once before, and she doesn't want to let him down again by giving in to the likes of Maurice Warner.'

'What happened to her boyfriend?' Rebecca asked.

'Oh, he just moved on; he found a job up the country somewhere, a few weeks later, and hasn't been heard of since,' Laurence told her. 'Some people said, "Poor Hazel! What got into her at all?" But who knows if she made the right decision? If she didn't love him, she just couldn't marry him. Other couples must have their doubts too, sometimes, but it had to be all or nothing as far as Hazel was concerned.'

Rebecca was deep in thought. She was glad Laurence had told her about Hazel's unhappy past; sympathy was the last thing in the world her aunt would want from her, but at least now Hazel's mood swings didn't seem so unreasonable after all.

Some time later, Maurice Warner drove up the drive-way to John Coakley's front door. Now that he knew that John Coakley's wife would much prefer to be living in Killarney, he'd decided to offer them a sweetener.

John was in his mid-thirties, his eyes a greyish colour that added to their intensity. He stood in his big blue living-room and listened to what his visitor had to say.

'You'll have to admit my offer is a fair one,' Maurice said. 'It's not as if I'm trying to cheat you out of some-thing that's rightfully yours.'

'I never said you were,' John reminded him. 'It's just that I'm not interested in selling, and I've told you so before.'

'Yes, I appreciate that,' Maurice assured him. 'But what if I were to offer you something extra — like a house in an estate in Killarney? There's a very nice one here in Briarwood.'

John eyed him resentfully as he opened a brochure and laid it on the table. He knew at once what this was all about. Warner had done his homework and was trying to get at him through his wife, Hannah, who was listening in silence in the background.

'It's a very nice estate, very pleasant. I've driven round it more than once, and the houses are all very well-maintained,' Maurice continued. 'As you can see from the photographs, they've got good-sized gardens at the rear.'

'I don't care if they've got fifty acres at the back, I'm just not interested,' John insisted. 'I've put a lot of sweat into trying to make a go of this place, and I'm not going to throw it all up now. We left the town a long time ago, and we're not going back.'

'Do you know the price of houses in Killarney?' Maurice asked, his expression more serious still.

'You're not just getting a very good deal here, you're getting a brilliant one.'

'That may be so; but I'd say, Mr Warner, you're not the type to give anyone a free dinner,' John countered. 'You wouldn't be offering what you're offering unless you were planning to make the same and more in double-quick time.'

'Oh, people who invest in trees have to learn to be patient,' Maurice assured him. 'Even with the fast-growing spruces, you're talking about a few years before I'd get any return on my investment.'

He focused on the brochure again. 'Wouldn't you at least go in and have a look at the house? What would you have to lose?'

John sighed. He'd say one thing for Warner: he didn't give up easily.

'There wouldn't be any point. How many times do I have to tell you we're not interested in selling?'

'And does your wife feel the same way?' Maurice asked, turning to her. Hannah Coakley made no reply.

'Look, we've given you our answer,' John said, trying hard to disguise the frustration in his voice.

'Well, I'll leave you the brochure anyway, in case you change your mind,' Maurice said.

As he drove off, John's youngest daughter, ten-year-old Ella, came in from the back yard. 'What did he want?' she asked.

'What do you think? The man just can't take no for an answer,' her father told her.

But already her mother was poring over the photographs of the house in the brochure. 'He's right,' she said. 'Briarwood is much nicer than our last place in Killarney. It's a cul-de-sac, too, which means you get very little traffic.'

'I'd hate to live in the town,' Ella said. The family

had moved back to Dereenard before she was born.

'Maybe you would and maybe you wouldn't,' her mother replied. 'It isn't as if you'd be short of open spaces. The national park is just a stone's throw away, and you can't get much bigger than that.'

'The difference is that we've owned the land here for generations. And I'm not going to let some slick, glib trick-merchant like Maurice Warner get his hands on it now,' John vowed.

Hannah looked at him. She heard the determination in his voice. In many ways he was a quiet, easy-going man; he kept his thoughts to himself and didn't lay down the law for anyone. The only thing that put him on the defensive was the thought that he might lose the farm. And, of course, she could understand how he felt; but the fact was that she was bored around the house, and she missed the companionship of her work-mates at the hotel.

'But, John, it wouldn't do any harm to have a look at the house,' she ventured.

'Are you mad? If we so much as set foot inside that gate, he'll think he has us hooked and we'll never get rid of him,' John countered. 'So, for goodness' sake, will you put Warner and his house right out of your mind?'

He returned to his chores, and Ella glanced at the brochure. She could see the longing in her mother's eyes; but she hoped, desperately hoped, that her mother wouldn't go and view the house on her own.

Sam owned the horses, but during the summer months, when they finished their work in the evening, they grazed in fields rented from the Coakleys. Later that evening, when Rebecca went to see the horses, she met Ella for the first time. Ella was preparing to groom Rafferty with brushes and combs. This was something she loved to do, and she was only too happy to allow Rebecca to help her.

'Laurence and his cousin groom the horses themselves, but I give them an extra treat like this every now and then,' Ella told Rebecca.

'I hope I'm doing it the right way,' Rebecca said, as she moved the brush over Rafferty's coat.

'Oh, Rafferty's not too fussy, as long as you're gentle with him. I've been doing it for ages, and I'm still not sure if I go the right way about it,' Ella admitted. 'All I know is that he seems to enjoy it.'

'Yes, he looks happy, all right,' Rebecca agreed. Rafferty's tail was swishing lazily.

Ella told Rebecca about the visit from Maurice Warner; she was still troubled about it.

'Your father won't sell,' Rebecca said, though she couldn't help remembering what Laurence had said: he wouldn't count on John Coakley sticking to his guns.

'It isn't that simple,' Ella replied gloomily. 'My father borrowed money from the bank, you see, to make improvements on the farm. He's paid back some of it, but he still owes them a lot.'

'But as long as he's paying them back, even little by little, they'll give him time, won't they?' Rebecca said.

'I don't know,' Ella replied. 'He hates being in debt. He doesn't talk about it much — at least, not to me — but I'm sure he thought he'd have the balance paid off ages ago. And the last thing he needs is the likes of Maurice Warner stirring up trouble for him.' Rebecca liked Ella for being so honest, but she could hear the anxiety in her voice. 'If the bank hears he's been offered a good price for the place, they mightn't go so easy on him; and sooner or later Mr Warner's bound to make it his business to see that they do hear it.'

'If your father did sell out, where would the horses graze for the summer?' Rebecca asked. 'The Murphys' place and Dan Quigley's have already been sold, and Hazel has so many sheep that she hardly has enough grass as it is. Besides, her land isn't nearly as good as this.'

'Oh, I couldn't bear the thought of Rafferty and Star and the others having to go somewhere else! They're my friends and I'd miss them like anything,' Ella said, and it seemed as if her anxiety had given way to despair. 'Rafferty's the best at his work, but he's a bit of a pet, too. I have to buy lump sugar specially for him because he loves it. The woman in the shop in Killarney probably thinks we're very posh, buying lump sugar.'

Rebecca smiled, but in a moment she and Ella fell silent again. The future of the forestry horses seemed more uncertain than ever; but was there anything either of them could do about it?

Chapter Five

'Timber!' Laurence called out, as another tree came crashing down. He didn't really like to see the trees being felled, he admitted; but the fact that they were replaced almost at once with new saplings meant that the forestry would always be a green and living place.

Rebecca was working on her sketch of Rafferty again; she really wanted it to be something special.

'I've some news for you,' Laurence smiled, when she took a break for a moment. 'Sam wants to buy your sketch. He wants to frame it and hang it up in his office.'

'What!' Rebecca exclaimed in surprise and delight.

'So from now on you can't say you're not an artist. Anyone who's sold a picture is an artist,' Laurence told her.

'But Sam hasn't even seen it yet,' Rebecca reminded him. 'He mightn't like it.'

'He'll like it, all right. Besides, I've told him it's very good,' Laurence assured her. 'Come to think of it, I should get some sort of commission. I'm like your agent, amn't I?'

Rebecca laughed. She knew he wasn't being serious. 'I'd love to see it framed,' she admitted, glancing at the sketch again.

'And you can be sure that when anyone calls to the office, Sam won't let them out the door again without telling them about it,' Laurence predicted.

At that very moment, Sam was playing host to Helen Heffernan, the Managing Director of Heffernans Builders Providers.

'I'm sorry about all that bother with my great-nephew,' Sam apologised, handing his guest a cup of coffee. 'He takes things too much to heart, and he gets hot under the collar at times.'

'We all have bad days, Sam, but we don't take it out on the customers,' Helen said. 'If we did, it wouldn't be long before we had no customers left.'

'Oh, I'm sure Matt regrets what he said. He's quick-tempered, but at the back of it all he's a good worker,' Sam explained.

'Well, if it was any other company but yours, I'd have taken my business elsewhere straight away,' Helen replied. 'I didn't do it because you and my father — well, you go back a long way.'

'That we do,' Sam agreed. 'Your father loved nothing better than to go up to the forestry and have a look at the horses at work.'

'That said, Sam, no one can run a business on

sentiment — at least, not these days,' Helen told him. 'I know ordering special lengths and the like makes life difficult for you. It makes life difficult for us, too, but it's what our customers want.'

'Oh, I understand all that; and you can take it from me, you'll get exactly what you want,' Sam assured her.

'Now, about the price, Sam....' Helen went on.

Sam eyed her closely. She was a tough customer, but he couldn't help admiring her all the same. He envied her father for having someone like her to take charge when he wanted to take things a bit easier.

Some time later, Sam accompanied Helen across the yard to her car.

'A pleasure to do business with you, Helen,' he said, shaking her by the hand.

'And with you, Sam,' she replied, before getting into the car and driving off.

A moment later, Matt came striding towards his great-uncle. 'What the hell was she doing here?' he snapped. 'I thought I told her in no uncertain terms that I couldn't supply her at the prices she wanted.'

'And I thought I asked you to ring her back and say you'd changed your mind, but you just stormed out on me — again!' Sam replied, turning back towards the office.

'You rang her, didn't you?' Matt challenged him. 'You went behind my back and did a deal with her.'

'Well, someone had to do it when you wouldn't,' Sam said, his tone dismissive. 'The Heffernans are part of our bread-and-butter trade, our regulars, not people we hear from once in a blue moon.'

'And I suppose you told her to take no notice of Matt — he's still wet behind the ears, doesn't know his stuff,' Matt countered. 'Well, how do you think I feel now? I can never look that woman in the face again.'

'Oh, Matt, don't be so melodramatic. We all have to swallow our pride now and then,' Sam told him. 'If you'd gone to her yourself and apologised, like I told you, it would be so much water under the bridge.'

'Apologise? There was nothing to apologise for!' Matt insisted. 'But in future you can deal with her yourself. I've done my crawling when it comes to Ms Heffernan.'

'All right, Matt, all right,' Sam agreed. 'Now, like a good man, will you ever go back to whatever it was you were doing before?'

Matt said nothing, just walked away. He felt more resentful than ever. Sam treated him like some little errand-boy, and that was the way it would always be.

Just before lunch, Maurice Warner made a point of bumping into Matt on the street.

'Matt Staunton, isn't it?' Maurice said. 'I've heard a lot about you. Maurice Warner, Warners Wood Group. I was just about to go for a drink and have a bite to eat. Would you like to join me?'

The invitation took Matt by surprise, but after a moment's hesitation he accepted it. They made their way to The Lanterns, the local lounge bar, where Maurice ordered drinks and lunch for the two of them.

'You know something? I envy you, Mr Warner,' Matt confided, his blue eyes bright with emotion.

'Oh? Why is that?' Maurice enquired in his suave, reassuring way.

'Well, for one thing, you're your own man. You can make your own choices, stick with your own decisions,' Matt said.

'We all have to start somewhere, and everyone has someone on his case — even me,' Maurice replied. Matt looked at him in surprise. 'I'm supposed to be the Managing Director, but I have to square everything with my brother, and that's not always as easy as it sounds.' He lit a cigarette and took a drag. 'Besides, if you want to do an apprenticeship in the forestry trade, you couldn't pick a better man than Sam Staunton — or so they tell me.'

'Do they?' Matt replied, unconvinced. 'He has his own way of doing things, and if you don't go along with it, you're in big trouble.'

Their conversation was interrupted for a moment as a waitress came to the table with their meal.

'The atmosphere can be stifling,' Matt went on. 'There's never any chance of doing something on your own initiative.'

'There's nothing wrong with wanting to run a tight ship. You have to have someone who knows what everyone else is doing,' Maurice said. Again, he thought it best not to appear too critical of Matt's great-uncle at first.

'Then why does he bother to call me the Manager when he knows it's little more than a title?' Matt persisted.

'Families are great, always there when you need them,' Maurice mused; 'but maybe it's like me and my brother — maybe it's best to keep them at arm's length when it comes to business.'

'Exactly,' Matt agreed. 'When I started off, I had great plans to shake things up a bit; but now I'm sorry I took the job in the first place.'

'Well, if you ever decide you want to get out, give me a buzz. We're always looking for bright young people at Warners,' Maurice said.

'Do you really mean that?' Matt asked, taken by surprise.

'Of course I mean it. I never say anything I don't mean,' Maurice assured him.

Hazel was a sheep farmer, but she also kept some goats and made cheese from their milk. A few days later, Rebecca watched with interest as her aunt set to work in the small dairy at the back of the farmhouse.

'Some people don't like goat's cheese; they say it's too strong,' Hazel told her. 'But then, I don't have that much to sell, and the health shop in Killarney would take more if I had it.'

'It's a taste you'd have to get used to, all right,' Rebecca agreed; she had already tried some of her aunt's produce.

'It has the goodness of the hills in it, if only people weren't so fussy and knew what was good for them,' Hazel replied.

She looked at Rebecca and turned to another subject. 'When Sam buys your sketch, I hope you won't fritter the money away — that you'll invest it wisely instead.'

'What do you think I should do with it?' Rebecca asked.

'Well, if it was me, I'd get myself a set of really good brushes and paints,' Hazel suggested. 'It's like everything else: you have to go about it the right way if you want to make an impression.'

Luke Moran appeared in the doorway. Hazel frowned, making it plain at once that she had no great welcome for him.

'I suppose there wouldn't be a bit of cheese going?' he began, in his roguish way.

'There might be,' Hazel replied, cutting a chunk and handing it to him. Rebecca observed him closely as he ate the cheese. She didn't like him very much because Laurence had accused him of beating Star.

'I'm thinking it won't be long till you're the only one left in the place, Hazel,' said Luke. 'Warner is after offering the Coakleys a house in Killarney, and Coakley's missus is after looking around it. She's right taken with it — mighty taken, so she is.'

'How do you know that?' Hazel demanded, unimpressed. Luke often made statements that were highly coloured or exaggerated.

'Didn't she give me a lift, just a while ago?' Luke countered. 'It's a grand house, she says — double-glazed windows and the devil knows what. It would suit her down to the ground.'

Rebecca began to dislike Luke even more. Not only was he trying to antagonise Hazel, he was also trying to make her feel more insecure and isolated.

'And that's not all. She called around to a few hotels, and she could get work in the morning if she wanted it,' Luke smirked, a kind of gloating in his green eyes. 'When Mr Warner calls again, can't you ask for the same thing — a house in Killarney on top of the money he's offering you?'

'Whatever about anyone else, Luke, I'm not moving anywhere,' Hazel assured him, as she wrapped a block of cheese in some muslin. 'So if you happen to see Mr Warner on your travels, you might like to save him a journey by telling him that nothing he could offer me would make the slightest difference.'

'Ah, now, Hazel, never say never,' Luke chided. 'No one can predict what will happen in the future.'

Hazel made no reply, but when Luke was gone she had plenty to say.

'You know what he's doing, don't you? Stirring the pot,' she snapped. 'That man loves to see commotion between his neighbours.'

'He wasn't very nice to the horses, anyway,' Rebecca replied.

'Oh, the world and his mother knows he has it in for Sam, ever since Sam gave him the push,' Hazel agreed. 'And he'd love to see me brought down a peg or two, as well.'

Rebecca looked at her curiously; she didn't understand.

'It was a good few years ago. My father wasn't well, and Luke offered to take a few sheep to the fair in Kenmare for him, to try and sell them,' Hazel explained. 'I must've been tied up with something else. Anyway, Luke sold the sheep, and my father was happy enough — until he met the buyer a few months later. It was a complete fluke that they ran into each other; but he found out that Luke had kept a nice slice of the money for himself.'

'That was mean,' Rebecca said with conviction.

'Yes, it was, especially as my father had insisted on paying him for his trouble,' Hazel replied.

'Has he any land of his own?' Rebecca asked.

'A small bit on the other side of the forestry,' Hazel told her. 'He used to do a bit of jobbing — buying and selling cattle, I mean — up to a few years ago; but now all he does is poke his nose into other people's business.'

Later that evening, Rebecca went to visit Ella. The tension in the Coakley house was palpable.

'My father and mother had a fierce row,' Ella confided, as she and Rebecca led the horses down to drink at the small lake that was part of the Coakleys' farm. 'My mother isn't talking to him now. So she looked around the house in Killarney — what's the big deal? Dad's right: Mr Warner's just using her to get at him.'

'Maybe he is, but your mother's never really liked the country, has she?' Rebecca said.

'No, she hasn't.... But I'm fed up with Mr Warner coming to the door every so often. Just when we think we're finished with him, he comes back again and causes more trouble,' Ella replied.

Sunlight winked on the surface of the lake, and Rebecca could almost sense the horses' anticipation as they longed for a cool, refreshing drink after their hard day's work.

'Hazel doesn't like Maurice Warner either,' she told Ella.

'My mother says Hazel is the cause of the whole trouble,' Ella said, and Rebecca admired her frankness. 'Hazel hates Warners, she says, but they've made Dad an offer that only a fool would refuse.'

They came to the lake at last, and the horses began to relish the coolness of the bright, clear water.

'I admire Hazel,' Rebecca said. 'She gets a bit moody sometimes, but working the land isn't just a job to her. She really loves the place, and she could never live anywhere else.'

'Oh, I admire her too,' said Ella. 'Mum's just looking for someone to blame.'

They stood in silence for a few moments, watching the horses drink from the lake. To Rebecca's surprise, Star went for a paddle, his eyes shining with pleasure as the water came up about his legs. She waited to see if Rafferty would join him, but he didn't seem inclined to.

As they stood beside the lake, the girls had no idea that the next day would be a day of high drama for Ella and her parents.

The postman placed a letter on the table, and John opened it casually as the postman was driving away.

'It's a solicitor's letter from the bank, reminding me that I'm behind with my repayments on the loan and warning me I'll be in big trouble if I don't cough up soon!' he exclaimed. 'Now what do you think of your civil Mr Warner?'

His wife made no reply.

'Didn't you hear me? What do you think of him now, I said?'

'Whatever I think or whatever I say will be wrong,' Hannah replied. 'And you've no way of knowing for certain that he had anything to do with this letter. It could be just coincidence.'

'Coincidence! If you believe that, you'll believe anything!' John scoffed. 'First it was the carrot and now it's the big stick. He's trying every dirty trick in the book to get his own way.' He crumpled the letter and flung it from him in disgust, then grabbed his jacket from the back of a chair.

'Where are you going? What are you going to do?' Hannah asked with mounting concern.

'I'll tell you what I'm going to do. I'm going to find your precious Mr Warner and I'm going to warn him I'll blow his head off with my shotgun if he ever sets foot on my property again,' John vowed.

'Oh, John, don't — don't go making threats. It'll only make things worse,' she pleaded.

'Are you afraid he'll withdraw his offer of the nice house in Killarney? Is that it?' he challenged her.

He didn't wait for a reply. In a moment he was sitting behind the wheel of the car, driving away.

He had never felt so angry in his life. They hadn't had a day's peace since Warner put his greedy eye on their land. It was like some sort of game to him; he was like an angler playing a fish until he tired him out and reeled him ashore at last. He'd met his match this time, though; Dereenard might be off the beaten track, but they weren't all backward gombeen men, as Warner might like to think....

These were the thoughts that raced through John's mind as he drove along the winding country road. He wasn't aware of it, but he was driving much faster than usual. Someone had to take a stand against Warner, or they'd never get him off their backs.... Sunlight flashed on the windscreen, blinding John's eyes, but this anger had been simmering inside him for a very long time and he was going to have his say, whatever the cost.

A sheep appeared out of nowhere, and he swerved to avoid it. The car went out of control and plunged headlong down the incline beside the road, finally coming to a stop when it struck a tree. Smoke began to billow from the engine. John slumped over the wheel, blood streaming from his forehead.

Some time later, a well-dressed man in a suit went scrambling down the hill to see if there was anything he could do. Maurice Warner had been driving along when he noticed the skid-marks on the road, and then the car crashed against the tree had caught his eye.

When he saw the blood on John's face, he gasped in horror. He dialled 999 at once on his mobile phone.

'Yes — yes, an ambulance. We need an ambulance on the Dereenard road, just a few hundred yards beyond the bridge,' he said urgently.

He opened the door of the car and tried to lift the driver from his place. It isn't the wisest thing in the world to move someone who has had an accident, but the smoke coming from the engine made Warner think the car might burst into flames at any moment.

He put John's arm about his shoulder and struggled to drag him to safety. Every second was vital — the pall of smoke was growing blacker and more ominous; but John felt so heavy, almost like a dead weight, in the heat of the afternoon. Warner gasped for breath, a kind of desperation in his eyes.

At last he managed to drag the unconscious man from the car. A moment later there was an explosive bang and flames shot up from the engine, engulfing the rest of the car in a matter of seconds.

When Warner had staggered a little distance away, he laid the injured man on the grass. He gasped again, this time more deeply. There were bloodstains on his suit, and they filled him with horror. If only the ambulance would come — and come soon!

Chapter Six

*T*he news about John's injuries was uncertain at first. Hazel went to visit him in hospital a day or two later, and was told by Hannah that he might have to use a wheelchair.

'He'll never survive if that happens — a man who was used to being always out and about,' she said, struggling to hold back the tears. 'I can't tell you how relieved I was when he regained consciousness, but he says he has no feeling at all in his lower limbs.'

The two women were on their way out of the hospital, heading for the car park.

'The car was a write-off, of course, but who cares about that?' Hannah continued. She no longer felt any resentment towards Hazel; the accident had changed everything. 'But now that I don't have a car of my own, you see why I had to move into the house in Briarwood. I couldn't be scrounging lifts off people all the time, and I want to spend as much time as I can with John. And it's great for the boys, too, having a place of their own to come home to in the evening instead of having to share with strangers.' Ella had two older brothers, one in secondary school, the other at college, both working in Killarney for the summer.

Hannah paused and looked at Hazel more seriously still. 'It's very nice of you to let Ella stay with you for a while,' she said.

'Oh, no trouble at all,' Hazel assured her. 'It's nice for Rebecca to have someone her own age about the place. I must admit I'm not the best of company at times.'

'Ella's like her dad, like a fish out of water in the town,' Hannah said.

'And the animals are fine. The girls and Laurence and I have been keeping an eye on them,' Hazel reassured her.

'You're all very good,' Hannah said. 'And Mr Warner couldn't have been nicer. It was a lucky thing he came along when he did. Otherwise John would've burned to death in the car.'

This praise for Maurice Warner grated on Hazel, but she resisted the impulse to contradict it. People were talking about Warner as if he were some kind of hero, but he had only done what anyone else would have done in similar circumstances; and John wouldn't have been on the road in the first place if the letter from the bank hadn't goaded him into driving off at high speed in search of the self-same Mr Warner. All that, however, was conveniently forgotten in the blinding glare of Warner's newly sprouted halo. People could be so fickle!

'You know, he's right, though,' Hannah resumed, as she got into Hazel's car — Hazel had offered her a lift to the estate at Briarwood. 'No matter what happens,

John won't be able to work the place the way he has up to now. John's like you, Hazel — very independent; he couldn't bear the thought of having to depend on other people to do most of the work for him. Besides, there's the money we owe the bank.... We couldn't really afford to hire someone.'

'There's always a way of getting round problems if you put your mind to it,' Hazel insisted.

'I wish I had your strength, Hazel!' was all Hannah said in reply; but Hazel sensed that, now she'd made the move to Briarwood, she'd never go back to Dereenard again — which meant that Maurice Warner would have his greedy hands on her husband's farm sooner rather than later.

'I was afraid he'd reduce his offer or renege on it after what happened to John, but I was wrong. He's a man of his word, he says, and his offer still stands,' Hannah said, confirming Hazel's suspicions.

Maurice Warner sat in his office and picked up the telephone again.

'The Coakley place is as good as ours,' he assured his brother, wisps of smoke curling from the cigarette he held in his hand. 'And the best part of all is that I seem to be as welcome as the flowers of May wherever I go.'

'But what about the old man, Sam Staunton?' Philip asked.

'I've offered his great-nephew Matt a job, but I don't want to put him under too much pressure,' Maurice explained. 'He's so uptight; he's like a rope that's stretched to the limit and ready to snap.'

'Even if he does walk out on the old man, will it

make any difference?' Philip asked.

'Maybe not at first, but Sam can't keep going for-ever,' Maurice replied.

'We can't wait that long,' Philip reminded him.

'Oh, I'm sure I'll think of something to give the old man a nudge in the right direction,' Maurice said, and his words had an ominous ring to them.

'Whatever you do, make sure it doesn't reflect badly on the company. The last thing we need is bad publicity,' his brother warned.

'I'll make it my business to see that no one can point the finger of blame at us. But then, like I say, it may not even come to that,' Maurice assured him.

'That only leaves that woman, Hazel Cronin,' said Philip.

'Yes, and she's proving to be the most troublesome of all,' Maurice replied. 'She has this thing about holding on to her land for the sake of her father. He died a few years back, but his ghost still seems to haunt her.'

'And is there nothing you could offer her that might make her change her mind?' Philip asked.

'That's what I'm trying to find out,' Maurice said. 'I offered to buy her land somewhere else and give her a fair exchange, but she wasn't interested. It seems to be a case of Dereenard or bust, as far as she's concerned.'

'Well, then, you do have a problem, Maurice,' Philip told him.

When Maurice replaced the receiver, he sank deep in thought. Something Luke had said occurred to him again. Hazel was a wizard at mending bits of machinery, as good as any mechanic; that was part of the reason she refused to part with her old banger of a tractor. She loved messing around with it.

Maurice smirked to himself.

The trouble with a tractor like that was that something could go wrong when it was least expected. The brakes could easily fail, for instance....

Here was a little job for Luke. Luke was one of those people who nursed grudges against almost everyone around him. And if he ever felt an urge to talk about his adventures, there would be ways and means of silencing him.

One evening, Laurence stood by Hazel's side as they looked towards the Coakleys' now-unoccupied home.

'I know John couldn't help having his accident, but sometimes I find myself wanting to blame him,' Hazel admitted. 'I feel as if I've been deserted left, right and centre — first by the Murphys, then by Dan Quigley and now by the Coakleys.'

She turned to glance at Laurence. 'And you needn't try and tell me the Coakleys won't really sell; it's only a matter of days. John's very down in the dumps — but then, you could hardly blame him.'

'But you won't sell and Sam won't sell, and that's all that matters,' Laurence said. 'Maurice Warner said he wouldn't go ahead with his plans unless he could get his hands on all the land from the forestry to your place.'

'You have to hand it to him, don't you? I mean, the way he goes about his business,' Hazel said. Laurence looked at her curiously. 'The way he finds some weakness and exploits it. That's how he manages to pick people off one by one.'

'You make him sound like a sniper or something,' Laurence said.

'I would've said a vulture,' Hazel replied, her tone as serious as before.

Their conversation was interrupted as Rebecca came running towards them.

'Come quick, Laurence, come quick! There's something wrong with Rafferty!' she gasped.

'What's the matter with him?' Laurence asked with sudden concern. He ran with her down the sloping field towards the lake.

'He's snorting and coughing, and there's something wrong with his breathing.'

'Oh, damn — maybe I've been asking him to do too much in this hot dry spell,' Laurence said. 'He's not getting any younger; but he's always so willing, and he likes to feel he's done a good job.'

'It isn't your fault. You couldn't be nicer to him,' Rebecca gasped.

They came to Ella, who was crouching over Rafferty as he lay on the ground.

'He's going to be all right, isn't he? He's not going to die?' she asked apprehensively. She'd always been fond of the horses, but since her father's accident she'd grown still closer to them.

'I don't know — I don't know. We can only hope,' Laurence replied. 'I don't like the sound of that wheezing, and his breathing's a bit strained.'

He patted Rafferty reassuringly, the sunlight warm and bright in the horse's dark eyes. 'One of you run up and ask Hazel to phone the vet. We won't move him till we hear what Jill says.'

'I'll go this time,' Ella volunteered, and she set off racing up the incline.

'Have you any idea what it could be?' Rebecca asked. She knew that Laurence knew a great deal about horses, having worked with them for so long.

'I'm not sure, but there's one thing I'm hoping it's not, and that's equine flu,' Laurence replied, frowning with intensity.

'Why? What's that?' Rebecca asked.

'It's a very severe infection caused by bacteria, and sometimes it's fatal,' Laurence told her.

It seemed as if Rebecca and Laurence crouched over Rafferty, waiting for the vet, forever. Rebecca glanced at her watch now and then, but that only made the time drag more slowly still. Again she sensed the warm bond of friendship and companionship that Laurence and Rafferty shared; there was a gentleness in Laurence's touch that could not be mistaken.

At last they saw the young vet hurrying down the hillside towards them, Ella by her side. Rebecca and Laurence moved back to let the vet carry out a thorough examination of her patient.

'What's wrong with him, Jill?' Laurence asked at last.

'I'm not exactly sure what it is,' the vet admitted. 'It could be just a chill, or it could be something more serious. I'll give him something to help him with his breathing and ease the inflammation in his throat.'

She removed a syringe from her bag and injected Rafferty with a clear liquid. 'This will make him drowsy soon, so we'll have to get him up to one of the outhouses as quick as we can. He'll probably be a bit unsteady on his legs, but I think he should be able to manage it under his own steam.'

Laurence encouraged Rafferty to rise to his feet, and, as always, Rafferty responded to his encouragement. 'Oh, you're a great man, a great man,' Laurence assured him as he struggled from the ground, his breathing becoming still more laboured. 'Don't you fret, now. We'll have you as right as rain in no time at all.'

'All you can do for the time being is let him rest and

keep him warm, because his temperature is almost feverish,' Jill told Laurence as they made their way slowly up the hill.

'My father says it's good for a horse to sweat the badness out of him,' Laurence said, as if struggling to reassure himself that Rafferty would really be all right.

When they came to the outhouse, they found that Hazel had been busy too, brushing out a stall and laying down clean straw, on top of which she had spread out some blankets.

'Oh, this is perfect, Hazel — fine and roomy. He'll be snug and warm in here and still have plenty of air,' the vet said as she looked about her. 'And, by the looks of things, he'll have two very attentive nurses, too,' she added, glancing at Ella and Rebecca.

Hazel agreed that the two girls could set up make-shift beds in the outhouse and spend the night with Rafferty. They couldn't sleep, however, so they spent much of the night simply sitting close to Rafferty.

'Everything's gone wrong this summer,' Ella said. 'In a few years' time, I'll be a stranger in Dereenard, and even our house will be gone.'

'Maybe things won't work out the way you think they will,' Rebecca suggested. 'If Hazel holds her ground, Mr Warner will have to give up on his plans for the place.'

Jack was restless too. Sometimes he sprawled on the ground and tried to sleep, but then he rose again and began to sniff at Rafferty's head. Rafferty moaned and groaned now and then, and Rebecca and Ella were filled with unease.

'If anything happens to Rafferty, it'll be the end of the forestry horses,' Ella said, voicing her worst fears at last.

'What makes you say that?' Rebecca asked.

'Rafferty's the oldest and most experienced, and Laurence says he does the work of two of the others put together,' Ella explained. 'It isn't just that, though. If he didn't get better, a new young horse would have to be trained and broken in. That would take time and money, and Sam might think it just wasn't worth the bother or the expense.'

'But Sam loves the horses,' Rebecca reminded her. 'When I met him in the forestry the other day, he started telling me things about different horses that worked for his father and grandfather, down through the years. He can still remember all their names and the little habits they had, and why each one was special in its own way.'

'Oh, Sam loves the horses, all right,' Ella agreed. 'But Matt's never been keen on them. When he first took over as Manager, he wanted to get rid of them straight away, but Sam went against him. Now, though, things could be different — now that Rafferty's unwell. Sam wouldn't want to get rid of them, but if he and Matt had another argument, Matt might be the winner.'

Rebecca was more troubled than ever. The horses were as much a part of the forestry as the trees themselves, and if they were replaced by machines, the woods of Dereenard would never be the same again.

The girls lay on their blankets and tried to sleep again. The air was heavy and oppressive, and still they tossed and turned, but at last their eyelids drooped and closed.

Laurence came back at the crack of dawn. 'Poor man, he doesn't seem to be much better,' he said, rubbing his hand through his hair, as he sat in Hazel's living-room. 'I don't know what I'd do if anything happened to him. I couldn't bear it if Jill said she'd have to put him down.'

'Well, she hasn't said that, and she won't,' Hazel said firmly. 'Many an animal has been in a fever for a week and pulled through in the end.'

'People will tell you that you shouldn't get senti-mental about a horse, especially a working horse — but how could you not get sentimental about a horse like Rafferty?' Laurence asked. 'It's a pleasure to go to work in the morning, because no matter what goes wrong, you know you can always rely on Rafferty.'

Jill came again. Rafferty's condition had worsened, but only slightly, and she said they shouldn't read too much into it for the time being.

Another day passed. Laurence divided his time between the outhouse and the kitchen. He phoned Sam and told him what had happened. Of course it would be all right if he took a few days off work, Sam said, when he came to visit Rafferty himself.

'He's burning up, and there's nothing we can do,' Laurence said. He was sitting in the kitchen again, watching the pendulum in the clock swing relentlessly backwards and forwards. 'This reminds me of when I was a child. I had a dog, and he became very sick. I prayed and prayed and promised God I'd do all sorts of good things, but still he died.'

'Laurence, do you remember my father was a great man for the herbs? I still have his notebook, and there's a recipe in it for a potion that might do Rafferty some good,' Hazel suggested abruptly. 'If he hasn't improved in the morning, why don't you go out and find some of the herbs? It would give you something to do — and who knows, if all goes well we mightn't need to use the potion at all.'

Morning came; Rafferty was still no better. Laurence searched for the herbs in the fields. Hazel had given him a pocket guidebook, which helped him to identify those with which he wasn't familiar. Maybe he was clutching at straws, he thought, but sometimes the old ways were best.

At that very moment, Matt was confronting his great-uncle in the office again.

'This gives us the perfect excuse to hire a small timber harvester for a week or two — and then you can make up your own mind whether it's better than the horses or not,' he said.

'Seems to me you've already made up your mind on that score,' Sam replied. 'Anyone would think you were glad the horse is laid low.'

'That's not fair,' Matt protested. 'All I'm saying is that now we've a chance to do things my way for a change. Even if Rafferty does get better, he'll need time to recuperate; you can't just send him back to work tomorrow or the day after. And if things don't work out with the machine, you can get rid of it again.'

'I don't know,' Sam said uncertainly. 'Laurence won't like it. He's dead against machines; he says they do too much damage.'

'So what if Laurence doesn't like it?' Matt snapped. 'He's not the boss. You are — though sometimes I wonder who's running the show around here.'

'And what's that supposed to mean?' Sam challenged. He knew that Matt was jealous of his relationship with Laurence; he and Laurence both had an affection for the horses that Matt simply didn't understand. Accounts and figures and invoices were the only things Matt understood.

'I know Laurence is the golden boy around here and we can't say a word against him, but a little bird told me how he hit the bottle when his brother was drowned,' Matt retorted.

'That's all in the past, and don't you go dragging it up again, do you hear me?' Sam warned him. 'Laurence did everything he could to save his brother, but people with wagging tongues — people like Luke Moran — made out that his rescue attempts were only half-hearted because he and his brother were always jealous of each other.' Sam looked at Matt more closely, an unfamiliar sternness in his expression. 'No wonder he hit the bottle, with gossip like that doing the rounds.'

'Oh, don't get me wrong. I've nothing against Laurence,' Matt told him. 'It's just that I'm getting sick of people worrying about what he might or mightn't think all the time.'

'Do you know something, Matt? You can be very petty when you like,' Sam snapped. 'But all right — we'll play it your way this time. You can hire your machine for a week or two. But take it from me, the minute Rafferty recovers, he'll be back on the beat again.'

Matt resisted the impulse to point out that there was very little point in hiring a machine if Sam's mind was already closed against its possible advantages. On the other hand, this was the first time Sam had agreed to allow a machine into his forestry; and that in itself was a small but significant victory. A great deal could change in the space of a few weeks.

Chapter Seven

A few days later, Rafferty was on the mend. Laurence insisted that Hazel's herbal remedy had played a big part in his recovery.

'I added a spoon or two of honey so the stuff wouldn't taste so bad,' Hazel explained, as they fussed over Rafferty.

'He's breathing a lot better, anyway,' Laurence said, and there was joy and relief in his voice. 'A few more days and he'll be as right as rain, though when he goes back to work he'll have to take things easy for a while.'

'But what about the new machine?' Ella asked, with some concern. 'Didn't your cousin tell you Sam was fairly impressed with it?'

'All Sam said was that the man with the machine was a good honest worker — nothing more, nothing less,' Laurence replied. 'When it comes to a choice between Rafferty and the machine, you can be sure

Sam will choose the right way.'

'Well, I must be off. There's work to be done,' said Hazel.

As she got behind the wheel of the tractor, Jack began to bark with unexpected vigour.

'It's all right, Jack, I haven't forgotten you. Come on, jump up here beside me,' Hazel told him.

Jack refused to do as she said; he continued to bark with the same urgency as before.

'What's got into you this morning?' Hazel wondered, looking at him curiously. 'I've never known you to refuse a drive on the tractor before. But suit yourself.'

A few moments later, she turned in to a field — but as she drove down the incline, she discovered, to her horror, that the brakes had failed. Her heart missed a beat. She pressed on the brake pedal again and again, but there was no response. The tractor was plunging headlong down the hilly field; the low stone wall that enclosed the field was looming larger and larger.

'Damn and damn again!' Hazel exclaimed, her thoughts racing, her nerves pulsating. Now she knew why Jack had made such a fuss: he had sensed that something was wrong.

If she didn't make a jump for it, she would be thrown through the windscreen of the cab. She pressed on the brake more desperately still, in one last frantic effort; but it was futile. Hazel steeled herself a moment, then leapt from her place. She struck the hard dry ground with some force. The tractor careered on its way, crashing against the wall just seconds later.

Hazel was bruised and dazed, blood spewing from a gash below her right eye. Jack was running towards her down the hill, barking furiously; he sniffed about her, as she lay motionless on the ground, and began to whine with mounting concern.

Jack often took a notion to bark at the crows that sat on the telephone wires overhead, so it was some moments before Laurence and the girls came to investigate. Rebecca's heart began to pound as they rushed down the incline. She hoped against hope that Hazel wasn't badly hurt.

'Hazel? Hazel? Are you all right?' Laurence asked, a tremor of apprehension in his voice. Jack was still whining softly. 'Rebecca, run up and telephone the doctor.'

Rebecca did as she was told, and despite the fact that she was struggling against the hill, she ran faster than she had ever run before.

'I could carry her up to the house, no bother, but I don't want to move her in case there are any broken bones,' Laurence told Ella. Again, he seemed to be trying to come to terms with his own helplessness at a time like this. 'I'm hopeless in a crisis. I never know what to say or do.'

'You'd only make things worse if you did too much before the doctor came,' Ella assured him.

Laurence thought of his brother, who had drowned when they were both in their late teens. 'When I heard him scream for help, I ran up and down the strand like a headless chicken for ages,' he told Ella. 'I suppose I was afraid, a coward. You see, the tide was very strong, and he was a much better swimmer than me. In fact, he was better than me at most things, except maybe the horses.'

Ella made no reply. It seemed to be helping Laurence just to talk about things; it was a way of distracting himself from the present crisis for a moment or two.

'When I finally plucked up the courage and swam out to him, it was too late. People said there was a part of me that really didn't want to save him at all.'

'You know that isn't true, and that's all that matters,' Ella said.

The doctor came at last, and when he had examined Hazel, Laurence carried her up to the house.

Cuts and bruises, a sprained ankle, and a mild concussion; Hazel would feel sore for a while, but as long as she took things easy she would be fine again in a few days' time, the doctor said.

'Try to make sure she doesn't get worked up about anything,' he urged Rebecca.

'My head feels as if a ton of bricks fell on it,' Hazel said, when the doctor had taken his leave. 'I suppose I should've changed the tractor for a new one ages ago.'

'Oh, it's easy to be wise after the event,' Laurence said. 'Just stay in bed for a few days, like the doctor said.'

'I'll go mad if I stay in bed that long,' Hazel protested. 'I've a million things to do.'

Only an hour or so later, Hazel had a visitor.

'You do pick your moments, Mr Warner,' she told him bluntly.

'Oh, I'm sorry if I've come at an awkward time,' Maurice Warner said smoothly.

'Any time's an awkward time, as far as you're concerned,' Hazel snapped. 'So say what you've come to say and leave me in peace.'

'I'm willing to increase my offer, substantially increase it,' Warner told her with deliberate gravity, sitting down on a chair beside the bed.

'What, no little sweetener? No little inducements to sugar the taste?' Hazel countered, and he heard the jeering in her voice. 'How about a cabin cruiser? You must've heard I like to do a bit of fishing — but then, you've probably also heard that I'm not as easily impressed as other people.'

'The price I'm offering you is serious money,' he reminded her.

'Oh, I know it is. The only trouble is, I'm breaking even here and I don't have any debt troubles,' Hazel replied. 'If I had, you might be able to get my local friendly bank manager to turn the screws on me.'

'I could still make life very awkward for you,' Maurice told her.

'How?' Hazel demanded, unconvinced.

'Have you seen this week's edition of *The Kerryman*? Most people want my development to go ahead.'

'Oh, they do, do they? But then, it's not their land you want to buy,' Hazel reminded him.

'I've got public opinion on my side, and that's very important,' Maurice said. 'I'm holding a public meeting to explain my plans in detail — more jobs, not just in the forestry, but also in the sawmills. We're planning to expand them, you see.'

'Oh, are you?' Hazel jeered. 'I think Sam Staunton will have something to say about that. But I suppose I'll be the baddy at this meeting of yours, standing in the way of progress or some such nonsense.'

'I'm a very patient man, but even my patience is wearing thin,' Maurice told her more sternly. 'I've never let anyone stand in my way when it comes to business.'

'If that's some kind of threat, you needn't waste your breath,' Hazel replied. 'I've been around long enough to recognise a bully when I see one, so if you wouldn't mind, I'd like to take a rest now.'

'Yes, you have your rest — but I'd advise you to do some pretty hard thinking, too,' Maurice warned her as he rose from his seat.

Rebecca showed him to the front door and watched him drive away. Ella had gone off with Laurence to check on her father's animals.

When Rebecca went up to Hazel's bedroom, she could see her aunt was troubled.

'Is anything wrong?' she asked.

'That man will stop at nothing to get his own way,' Hazel said angrily. 'First it's the newspapers, and now it's a public meeting.'

'But they can't make you change your mind if you don't want to change it,' Rebecca said.

'I know that, but I can see him spouting some baloney about the forestry being the way of the future, especially on poor land like we have here in Dereenard,' Hazel predicted. 'He'll make it sound like he's doing us a favour.'

Rebecca sat down on the bed beside her.

'You must be sick of me and my problems,' Hazel said, but Rebecca assured her she wasn't. 'Warner thinks I've got some money tucked away, but I haven't. My father left most of his money to me when he died — he knew I was the only one interested in the place — but then, a few years back, Sam's business was going through a bad patch, and I couldn't bear to see him go under.'

'You mean you gave him a loan?' Rebecca asked.

'Yes. It was my idea, of course; Sam would never approach me for money — he's far too proud for that,' Hazel explained. 'But I knew he couldn't afford to go to the bank; the interest rates were crippling at the time. So I helped him out. He's paid me back some of the money, but he still owes me most of it.'

She smiled at Rebecca, a wistful smile. 'That's another reason why it's important to me that Sam shouldn't give in to Warner.'

When Rebecca went downstairs again, she was deep in thought. Hazel tried to give the impression that all she cared about was the sheep and the land, but her revelation about her loan to Sam confirmed again that she was capable of very deep friendships too.

Later that morning, Maurice gave Luke a lift in his car.

'I heard the little lady had a bit of an accident with her tractor,' Luke smirked.

'Yes, I heard something along the same lines, Luke; but you and I know nothing about it, do we?' Maurice warned.

'Oh, no, not a blessed thing, Mr Warner,' Luke assured him.

'So let's make sure it stays that way, for all our sakes,' Maurice said, a hint of menace in his voice.

'You can count on me. I can be very discreet, as you'd say,' Luke promised.

'I went to see her; she's a bit shaken, but still as determined as ever to stand in my way,' Maurice told him. 'So we may have to think of something else to give her a push in the right direction.'

'Like what?' Luke asked, his expression sly and curious.

'Like a brick through her window,' suggested Maurice. 'And I want you to try and stir things up at the meeting; make her look not just unreasonable, but stubborn and selfish too.'

'But if she's there herself, she'll tear me to pieces, man,' Luke said. 'You've never seen her when she's in a temper.'

'Oh, she won't be there. I'm the one who's called the

meeting, and she wants nothing to do with me,' Maurice said. 'So you'll have a free run. Get people worked up, so that at least one or two of them will say something extreme. Then, when the brick goes through her window, we won't have to look too far for suspects.'

'You're a clever man, Mr Warner,' Luke said, with admiration in his voice.

'Oh, I'm only getting into my stride, Luke. I've got something even more ·pleasant in store for the lady if she doesn't give in,' Maurice promised. Luke looked at him slyly, hoping he'd elaborate, but he didn't.

Soon the area was buzzing with the news that John Coakley had signed on the dotted line and sold his land at last. Ella was downcast, and Rebecca tried hard to cheer her up.

'It isn't the end of the world,' she said, as they led Rafferty from his stall. It was his first venture outdoors in weeks. 'You can always come and visit Hazel. I'm sure she'd like to have you.'

'Oh, Hazel's great — but it won't be the same, will it?' Ella replied. 'I'll have to go to a new school in September, and the townies will call me a culchie, a bog-trotter.... And what's my dad going to do all day when he comes home from hospital? He's never liked living in the town. And if he has to sit in a wheelchair, it'll drive him mad.'

'It won't be like that forever, Ella. When he's better he can look for work,' Rebecca said. 'They've got a farm and cows and stuff at Muckross, haven't they? Maybe he could get a job there. It wouldn't be the same as owning his own place, but it would be the next best thing.'

Rafferty was grazing in the field again, and even Ella couldn't resist a smile of pleasure.

'Things were looking bad enough for Rafferty a week ago, but look at him now. Things can get better. You can't give up hope, Ella,' Rebecca encouraged her friend.

'My dad's very depressed, though — and he's the sort that never gets depressed,' Ella confided.

'That's just the way he feels now. Who knows? He might feel different in a few weeks' time.' Rebecca smiled. 'So why don't you ask the people at Muckross about a job for him? It can't do any harm to try.'

'Maybe,' was all Ella said in reply.

Once the machine had begun to work in the forestry, Matt made a special effort to ensure that his great-uncle would decide to invest in a similar machine of his own. He rang round various companies in search of new orders; and just when it seemed that he was wasting his time, he struck it lucky. Whelans Providers were having trouble with one of their suppliers.

'We can never depend on them; they don't seem to know the meaning of the word "deadline". And that's no way to run a business,' said Mr Whelan's voice at the other end of the line. 'There's always some excuse, but it's come to the stage where we've had one excuse too many.'

'Well, if you'd like to try us for a change, I'm sure we can do better,' Matt promised with confidence.

'But you're a bit smaller than our regular suppliers.

Are you sure you could come up with the goods on time? After all, we don't want to go through the same hassle again,' Mr Whelan said.

'I'm sure we could meet your deadline. I won't say it wouldn't stretch us a bit, because it would, but we've invested in some new machinery lately,' Matt said. He knew this was something of an exaggeration, but he would have given anything to clinch the deal with Whelans, especially as Sam knew absolutely nothing about it.

'Oh, you've finished with the horses, have you?' Mr Whelan asked.

'Yes, yes. It was a bit of a wrench, but we thought it was time to move on,' Matt lied.

'Well, in that case, I can't see any reason why we shouldn't send some business your way. And if it works out, there will be more orders to follow,' Mr Whelan promised. 'I have your price list here, so I'll fax you our first order in an hour or so. All right?'

'That's perfect. A pleasure to do business with you, Mr Whelan,' Matt replied, and replaced the receiver.

He smiled with satisfaction and clenched his fists in triumph. This would prove to Sam, once and for all, that he could swing a deal with the best of them. The size of the order might stretch their resources to the limit, but if everyone worked flat out and Sam coughed up for a new machine, they could do it — he just knew they could.

When he received the fax, however, Matt was startled at the size of the order. And then there was the warning that the agreement would be cancelled if the goods were not supplied by the agreed deadline. Matt tried not to focus on this note of caution, but he found his mind drawn to it again and again.

Sam couldn't have been more surprised when his

great-nephew came to him and showed him the fax. Matt was beaming; Sam might have accused him of almost scuttling the deal with Heffernans, but he could make no such accusations this time round.

Sam looked down at the order and studied the details. 'Look, Matt,' he said, 'this would be great if they gave us a bit more time, but there's no way we could get all the stuff together by the deadline they've given us.'

'I might've known you'd say something like that,' Matt said accusingly.

'I'm not knocking the deal. I'd be the first to go for it if I thought we could honour it,' Sam said. 'But Whelans have always been a bit out of our league.'

'It's that kind of thinking that has us in the mess we're in,' Matt snapped. 'This could be the start of something really big, give us the boost we need, and all you can say is that we aren't up to it.'

'I'm trying to be realistic here,' Sam told him. 'If we take this order and can't deliver at the end of the day, we'll bring the whole place down around our ears.'

'That's a chance we've got to take — or are you afraid to take chances any more?' Matt asked. His blue eyes shone with resentment. 'It's those bloody horses again. We'll never make progress round here as long as they're tied round our necks like a millstone.'

'That's not right, and you know it. We wouldn't have a company if it weren't for the horses and their work down through the years,' Sam insisted.

'Then the time has come to make a break with the past. It's now or never, Sam, if you want this place to thrive,' Matt said urgently. 'Not so long ago, you'd have jumped at a chance like this.'

'Maybe I would, and I'll admit I'm tempted,' Sam replied.

'Well, don't take too long to make up your mind. If

we're serious about this order, we've got to get things up and running straight away — and the first thing that has to go is those horses,' Matt told him.

He left the office.

Sam mulled over what he had said. Maybe Matt was right; maybe he was too old for taking risks, he mused. He looked at the photographs on the facing wall, Rebecca's sketch of Rafferty taking pride of place amongst them. All those years when the horses had been at the very heart of things in the forestry.... But could Matt have the right idea? Could it be time for a change?

He took the fax in his hands and glanced through it again. If he had to get rid of the horses, it would be the hardest decision of his life.

Chapter Eight

*T*he public meeting called by Maurice Warner was held in the hall in the village. There was a good deal of interest in it. Warners were a big company and could be relied on not to renege on their promises, some people said.

'More jobs in the forestry and in the sawmills would mean more money in circulation, and that would be good news for everyone,' Maurice began, when he rose to his feet to address the crowd. 'Shops and pubs and petrol stations would all feel the benefit, not just the workers directly involved; it would be a breath of new life for Dereenard. And it could very well serve as a kind of magnet to attract further industries here.'

Luke, in the third row, smirked to himself. Anyone listening to Maurice would think he was some kind of saint.

'I know some of you will ask why we can't go ahead

with the project with the land we've already bought. Well, the simple answer is that it's a question of scale,' Maurice went on. 'When we do something at Warners, we like to do it right or not at all. We don't believe in starting up somewhere if there isn't a very real prospect that we can make a go of it. That's why we place so much emphasis on getting the groundwork right.'

There followed more of the same; but when Maurice came towards the end of his address, he tried to give the impression that the final decision rested with the people themselves.

'It wouldn't be right for me or anyone else to impose our views on you,' he concluded. 'It's your choice, and if we're not welcome here in Dereenard, then we'll simply have to look elsewhere to expand our business.'

Then the people in the hall were asked to give their opinions.

'There's always been a timber industry in Dereenard,' one man said, 'but if it isn't developed in the right way, it'll go to the wall, like a lot of other places before it.' This was music to Maurice's ears, and he smiled a kindly smile. 'We're living in the age of computers and cloning and virtual reality,' the man went on, 'and what we need more than anything else is new technology. It's the only way, if we want to fight off the competition.'

'Sam Staunton knows his trade well enough,' an old woman interjected. 'And why wouldn't he? He's been at it long enough. As long as he holds on to the horses, he has the best of both worlds: not only is he giving a good living to his workers, he's taking care of the environment into the bargain.'

This grated on Maurice, but still he smiled.

'I agree with the last speaker,' Laurence said, rising to his feet. Hazel had decided to boycott the meeting, but he had made it his business to attend; it would be

more than foolish to allow Maurice to have things all
his own way. 'The forestry horses have been part of the
scene in Dereenard for as long as anyone can remember,
and if we turn our backs on them now, we're going to
lose something very special.' Rebecca, beside him,
heard the emotion in his voice. 'The forestry horse is a
special breed: he's strong, he's proud, and he works
away quietly among the trees because that's the only
life he knows. He's been a friend to us down the years
and in tougher times than these. Today, more than
ever, he proves his worth, because he's a friend to the
environment too.'

'Ah, we're sick and tired of the likes of you giving
sermons about the environment,' Luke snapped, rising
from his place. 'What people want is jobs, not some
palaver about saving the planet. People need work
today — but then, you wouldn't understand. You've
had a steady job since you left school!' He smirked.
'Next thing we know, you'll be trying to persuade us
that one or two forestry machines will stop the little
birds from singing.'

'You tell him, Luke!' a fair-haired young man agreed.
'The rest of us would like a chance to go to work,
instead of sitting at home on our backsides all day. And
what's all the fuss about, anyway? A lousy bit of land
that's overrun by a flock of scrawny sheep.'

'The woman who owns the land doesn't look at it
like that, and she has every right to want to hold on to
her farm,' Laurence said.

Rebecca saw that the eyes of the fair-haired youth
who had risen in support of Luke were shining with
emotion too. 'That's the way it's always been around
here,' he insisted. 'The haves suit themselves, and to
hell with the rest of us! Well, it's about time the have-
nots like me had their say too.'

'Ah, you're wasting your breath, Jimmy. She's too selfish to think of anyone but herself,' Luke interrupted, egging the younger man on.

'You can't pin everything on Hazel. It's more than just land to her; it's a way of life,' Laurence protested.

'Tell her to sell up and give us all a slice of the action!' the fair-haired youth cried. 'And where is she tonight, anyway? Afraid to show her face in public, is she?'

Luke smirked to himself with satisfaction. He couldn't have cared less about Jimmy, or about jobs for the young people; all that mattered to him was putting old Sam Staunton and his cronies in their place for once in their lives.

Laurence and Rebecca went for an ice-cream after the meeting.

'I didn't make much headway there,' Laurence said.

'I thought you were very good,' Rebecca assured him, and he smiled.

'Do you know something that struck me recently? If any other place still had working forestry horses, they'd turn them into some kind of tourist attraction,' he said.

'It could still be done,' Rebecca said.

'Maybe it could, but it mightn't be the best thing for the horses themselves,' Laurence answered pensively. 'They'd become just another sideshow for the tourists, and their work wouldn't be real any more, if you know what I'm trying to say.'

Rebecca said she understood, but she could see how troubled he was.

He paused, rubbing his fingers round the rim of the glass that stood on the table before him.

'I don't know if I should tell you this, but I had a look at Hazel's tractor, and it looks as if it was tampered with,' he said slowly.

Rebecca looked at him in disbelief. 'You mean someone deliberately messed around with the brakes?'

'I can't be a hundred per cent sure, but it looks that way,' Laurence replied. 'It could've happened any time — while the two of you were down in the village or in Killarney or something.'

'But that would mean someone was watching us,' Rebecca said. It was a thought that filled her with unease.

Sam called to see Hazel the next day, and he was glad to see she was feeling much better.

'Are you sure it was me you came to see and not Rafferty?' Hazel joked, as she made him some tea.

'Well, I came to see Rafferty too,' Sam admitted.

He told her about the order he'd received from Whelans, and she smiled with delight.

'That's good news, isn't it?' she said.

'It would be if we could fill it on time; but even if Rafferty was on top form, we'd never achieve a target like that — at least, not with horses,' Sam replied.

'You're not thinking of getting rid of the horses?' Hazel asked, startled.

'I don't know what to do any more,' Sam admitted. 'And all I get from Matt is how fast a machine can operate and how fuel-efficient they are these days.'

'Some things never change, do they?' Hazel observed,

and he heard the criticism in her voice. 'You know as well as I do that the forestry wouldn't be the same without the horses; and even if Matt and his big machines made you a whole lot richer, you'd be a lot less happy too.'

'But there's your loan to think of, Hazel. You gave it to me in good faith, and it's about time I paid you back.'

'So that's what's troubling you? I should've known you wouldn't call just to enquire after my health,' Hazel laughed. 'I told you I trusted you; we agreed you'd pay me back whenever you could. That was good enough for me then, and it's good enough for me still.'

'I knew you'd say something like that, but I can't help feeling I'm being unfair to you, Hazel,' Sam said.

'Drink up, and come outside and have a look at Rafferty. Then tell me if you have any doubts about what you should do,' Hazel urged.

When they went outside, Rebecca was patting and stroking Rafferty; Ella had gone off with Laurence again, to check her father's stock.

'I've been telling him a secret,' Rebecca confided.

'What secret?' Hazel asked.

'If I tell you, it won't be a secret any more.'

'Ah, go on. You can trust us. We won't tell anyone else,' Sam promised. The very sight of Rafferty was enough to put him in a good humour again.

'I told him I really didn't want to come to Dereenard at first. I wasn't sure if I'd like it and stuff,' Rebecca told them. 'But now I think it's the best thing that ever happened to me, because it makes me feel special just to be his friend.'

Rafferty sniffed at her hair, and she rubbed his face with affection.

'Sam, I think you should thank Rebecca,' Hazel said.

'You see, Rebecca, he's been wrestling with his conscience, but I think you've settled an argument for him.'

Rebecca looked at her curiously. She didn't understand, but Hazel didn't elaborate.

When Sam returned to the office, he told Matt his decision: there was no way he could bring himself to replace the horses with machines, no matter how much sense it made to do so.

'Well, I've done my best and I can do no more,' Matt said with unusual resignation. 'I'll just have to try and find another job.'

'I know we've had our differences, but I'll be sorry to lose you,' Sam told him. 'You see the business as a career, and that's as it should be; but for me it's something more. It's friendship and family, and the horses too, all rolled into one. I hope you can try to understand.'

Matt's expression was not one of anger but one of weariness and regret. 'What I can't understand, Sam, is how you can look a gift horse in the mouth,' he said. 'I must've made fifty telephone calls before I struck it lucky with Whelans, and now it's so much time and effort down the drain.'

'They say you can't teach an old dog new tricks, and I'm beginning to think it's the same with an old horseman like me,' Sam replied. Then he wished Matt good luck for the future.

Matt found his jacket and put it on. Sam stood at the window and watched as he crossed the yard and made his way towards the gate. There was something inevitable about what was happening, and yet he could only feel sad that it had finally happened.

John Coakley began to show signs of improvement. There was some feeling in his legs again, and the doctors were very pleased with his progress. Ella decided to stay with her mother at Briarwood so that she could visit him more often.

Laurence took Rafferty to the blacksmith for a new set of shoes, and Rebecca went with them. She smiled with delight as they led Rafferty from the horsebox towards the forge. She sensed that Laurence saw the making of the new shoes as a kind of celebration.

In a little while she was trying her hand at the bellows. Con shaped the red-hot metal on an anvil, the blows of the hammer rhythmic and strong. Jack was with them too, and he eyed the man with the hammer curiously now and then.

Rebecca looked at Laurence; there was a quiet smile on his face. She remembered him saying that the clanking of Rafferty's harness in the forestry was like a kind of music to his ears. The pounding of the hammer against the anvil must be a kind of music to him too.

When she'd finished with the bellows, Rebecca patted Rafferty — so powerful, yet so patient — as he waited for the shoes to be fitted. Con lifted Rafferty's right foreleg and began to set the first of the shoes in place. He seemed different now, his face a mask of concentration, as if he was determined to ensure that everything was just right.

'You can't be too careful when you're putting new shoes on a horse,' he said, when he paused to catch his breath. 'If you make a mess of it, it's the horse that will suffer in the long run.'

He set to work again. When all the shoes were in

place, he put the hammer aside and removed his
apron, beads of sweat on his forehead. 'There now,
Rafferty. You'll feel like a new man after that,' he
promised. He lit a cigarette and took a drag of it.

'Matt came in for petrol a while back,' he said. 'I
asked him if he was feeling poorly or something, that
he wasn't at work, but he said he was after quitting.'

'That's bad news,' Laurence replied. 'Matt mightn't
win many prizes for diplomacy, but at least he's got
Sam's best interests at heart.'

'You never know, they might patch things up again,'
Con said.

'I wouldn't be too sure about that. Matt never
walked out before,' Laurence said, and now his tone
was gloomy.

The next day, however, Rafferty returned to work in the
forestry and Laurence was happy again. Star seemed
pleased to see Rafferty; it was as if he had been
wondering why his companion had deserted him all of
a sudden.

The sun blazed down and the temperature soared to
new heights, but the world of the forest was cool and
green. As soon as Rebecca had finished her breakfast,
she hurried off through the fields towards the trees. It
was a big day for her friends, and she wanted to be
part of it.

'I'm going to let him take it at his own pace. He'll
know when he's feeling fit again,' Laurence told her.
'He looks as proud as punch, doesn't he? Delighted to
be back in the harness.'

Rebecca nodded, and Jack barked his approval.

They walked with Rafferty as he made his way along the track, dragging the log that rested on the metal bar behind him. Sunlight flashed through the branches and shone on the horse's tackle, which Laurence had cleaned and polished with even greater care than usual. Everything seemed normal; even the birds were singing — but was it just an illusion? The thought filled Rebecca with unease.

Reality made its presence felt again the next morning, when Hazel discovered, to her horror, that someone had opened the gates during the night and the sheep were all over the road.

'Who'd have done such a thing?' Rebecca asked.

'Come on! Come on! There's no time for that now,' Hazel told her. 'We've got to round them up before there's an accident.'

Jack set to work, but the flock had scattered into twos and threes, and the freedom of the road seemed to make the stragglers more headstrong than ever. Rebecca and Hazel helped Jack as best they could, but the sheep leapt ditches or turned down side-roads, one sheep always heading one way and another heading the other.

'We'll never catch them all,' Rebecca thought gloomily as the morning wore on. But Jack never lost faith; he persevered in his task with a patience that rivalled Rafferty's. Rebecca panted and gasped. She couldn't remember when she'd done so much running before.

But at long last they began to make some progress, and the sheep grudgingly returned to their fields.

'Thank heavens for that,' Hazel sighed, when the

last of the strays had been rounded up and she had closed the gate behind them. 'It's very dangerous to have animals on the road. That's why I spend so much time keeping my fences in order.'

Rebecca struggled to catch her breath, and Jack panted furiously too.

'If I could get my hands on the swine that opened those gates, he'd think twice about doing the same again by the time I was through with him,' Hazel snapped, her tone bristling with resentment.

'Did it have something to do with the forestry and the way you refused to sell your land?' Rebecca wondered.

'Well, it's never happened before, and it's a bit too much of a coincidence that it should happen now — just when Mr Warner's been nice enough to come and tell me his patience is wearing thin,' Hazel replied.

Even though Rebecca couldn't help admiring her courage and resolve, she felt more uneasy still.

Later that night, when Rebecca and Hazel had just made their way up to their bedrooms, there was a crash of glass in the living-room below, and Jack began to bark with unusual viciousness. Rebecca's heart missed a beat.

Hazel came to her bedroom door. 'What the hell was that?' she asked.

They hurried downstairs again. Hazel opened the living-room door, and there before them was a brick on the floor, a gaping hole in the window and shards of glass strewn all around.

'Warner's really decided to up the tempo. He must be getting more desperate than I thought,' Hazel said. 'Be careful until I've brushed up the glass.'

She stooped to pick up the brick and found a note, hastily printed in pencil, attached to the underside: 'Get out and give the people jobs!'

'He must be getting the message that I intend to stick to my guns, if he's resorting to tactics like this,' Hazel said.

'But what if he does something really nasty? What then?' Rebecca asked, voicing her concerns at last.

'Oh, I'm sorry, Rebecca. Here I am just thinking of myself, and you must be feeling very afraid,' Hazel sighed. 'It isn't fair that you should get caught up in all this. Why don't you go and spend some time with Ella and Hannah in Briarwood?'

'No, no — I'd rather stay with you,' Rebecca insisted.

'Are you sure?' Hazel pressed, and Rebecca nodded. 'Well, to tell you the truth, I'm glad to have someone else around the place — another pair of eyes.' Hazel sighed. 'You see, the trouble with bullies is that you just can't give in to them, or they'll keep on doing the same thing over and over again. Someone has to make a stand.'

'I understand,' Rebecca assured her.

They began to clear up the glass. Rebecca glanced at Hazel, observing her closely. She seemed to be unshaken, taking it all in her stride; but was that just a disguise, a mask to hide her true feelings? Was she secretly very troubled and worried about what the future held in store?

When they had removed all the glass and placed some cardboard against the window as a temporary measure, Hazel made two mugs of cocoa. It would help them to sleep, she said.

But a little while later, Rebecca found herself tossing and turning in her bed. What if Hazel was right? What if Maurice Warner was becoming more desperate? That could only spell trouble for the forestry horses she had come to love so much.

Chapter Nine

*W*hen Rebecca visited the forestry the next morning, she found Laurence confronting Luke again.

'I thought I told you Sam doesn't want you around the horses after what happened before,' Laurence said.

'Steady on, Laurence, steady on. They won't catch some disease off me, if that's what's troubling you,' Luke jeered waspishly. 'I just thought I'd walk up and have one last look at them, for they'll soon be a thing of the past.'

'That's only wishful thinking, and you know it,' Laurence insisted. 'Yes, the horses have been part of our past, but they'll be part of our future too, if we have any sense.'

'Well, maybe you should ask young Matt Staunton what he thinks about that,' Luke jeered. 'In case you haven't heard, he's working for Maurice Warner now.'

This took Laurence by surprise, but he wouldn't

give Luke the satisfaction of hearing him translate that surprise into words. 'Matt's a grown man; he has to make his own choices, like the rest of us,' was all he said. 'And he's not the type to throw a brick through anyone's window,' he added, as an afterthought.

'Oh, I heard about that little affair,' Luke retorted. 'But, sure, some people are getting very annoyed with Hazel for holding things up.'

'One or two people are trying to make life difficult for her, I'll grant you that,' Laurence said coolly, 'but that's as far as it goes. And Hazel's more determined than ever to hold her ground.'

'It's a fright to be stubborn!' Luke said. 'She'd be doing us all a favour if she took the money Maurice Warner is after offering her a dozen times.'

'Are you expecting an executive post or something in the new set-up, Luke?' Laurence asked, a hint of mockery in his voice.

Luke glared at him resentfully. 'Go on, make your snide remarks and have your laugh. I'm used to it by now — not just from you, but from a great many more like you. But you can take it from me, Maurice Warner won't forget his friends at the end of the day.'

'If you think you're one of Warner's friends, you're even more naïve than I thought you were,' Laurence said. 'He put you up to making that little scene at the meeting, didn't he? But you don't have to be a genius to see he's just using you. When he's had his own way, when he's finished with you, he'll ditch you like so much unwanted baggage.'

'You'd better watch your lip, Connor,' Luke snarled. 'Nobody uses me or mine. Sam Staunton was the only one who ever tried to pull a stunt like that, but I soon put him in his place.'

'When did Sam ever try to use you?' Luke challenged.

'He gave me the roughest of the work up here, until in the end I had to take a stick to that useless nag.' Luke lit a cigarette and blew a smoke-ring. 'Oh, I haven't forgotten the way I was abused by Sam, though he took your word against mine every time.'

'I know you see all this as some sort of personal vendetta against Sam and Hazel, but it's much more important than that,' Laurence said, emotion rising in his voice. 'It's something that has implications for us all.'

'Especially for you and your precious nags,' Luke jeered. 'If I was you, I'd be making a few phone calls to the knacker's yard.'

Laurence grabbed Luke by the collar. 'It would give you some twisted kind of pleasure to see them slaughtered, wouldn't it, though they never did any-thing to you in their lives?' he said grimly.

'There's plenty of meat on them; I'm thinking they'd fill a good many cans,' Luke sneered. He was pleased that he'd goaded Luke into this display of anger, and he longed to make him angrier still. 'Sam mightn't get a great price for them — but, sure, at least he'd know all his good feeding wasn't after going to waste entirely.'

Rebecca was listening to every word, and the more Luke said, the more she disliked him.

'You're pathetic, Luke, do you know that?' Laurence said. 'So just clear off and keep out of my sight.'

'Oh, that's fighting talk, Mr Connor, fighting talk. But you haven't heard the last of Luke Moran, not by a long shot,' Luke retorted, pulling Laurence's hands off his collar and pushing him away.

Rebecca and Laurence stood in silence, watching Luke make his way down the path.

'He's as slippery as an eel; you never know which way he'll turn next,' Laurence said, and his words made Rebecca frown.

Later that day, Hazel and Rebecca went to visit Ella and her parents at Briarwood. John had been allowed home from hospital, but he was still in a wheelchair. Though he felt more hopeful that he would regain the use of his legs, he was still very depressed about the sale of his land.

'Why did you give in so easily, John?' Hazel asked, when Hannah had gone to make some tea in the kitchen. 'You knew you had friends; you knew we'd help you out.'

'That would have been all right if it was only for a short time, but I couldn't be a burden to people all my life,' John replied. 'Besides, I was never very happy about the notion of being in debt. It used to worry me all the time.' He looked at Hazel intently. 'It's very easy to sink so low you think you'll never climb up out of the pit again.'

'You don't have to tell me that, John,' Hazel assured him. 'I've been there myself. It was a long time ago, but it still hurts sometimes.'

'Anyway, if I can get myself together, I may be able to buy myself a small bit of land in time,' John said. 'And there's something else that came to me last night.'

Hazel looked at him curiously.

'If you stick to your guns, then my place at Dereenard won't be much use to Warners, and they'll probably put it on the market again.'

'That's a bit of a long shot, isn't it?' Hazel said. 'And even if they did, there's no guarantee your bid would be the highest.'

'That's where you're wrong, Hazel,' John told her. 'I've a very cute solicitor, and there's a clause in the agreement which says that if they put it on the market any time in the next five years, I must be given the first option to buy it back from them.' He smiled a wistful smile. 'To be honest, I didn't even know the clause was there till the solicitor told me about it. I suppose he could see I wasn't myself, and he was worried I might have serious regrets when the deal was done.'

Hazel praised the solicitor's foresight, but she felt under more pressure than ever. John was counting on her not to sell up; if she stood her ground, then there was a chance that he might be able to return to Dereenard.

A few evenings later, Rebecca was standing at the window when she thought she saw a shadow scurry across the yard.

Hazel had asked her to report anything suspicious, but it was very gloomy and she couldn't be sure what she'd seen. Should she go and investigate, or should she wait till Hazel got back from the village?

On impulse, she hurried towards the back door; but when she opened it, she hesitated again. What if there was some kind of danger out there in the shadows? She was no heroine when it came to things like this. She wished that Jack hadn't gone off in the car with Hazel, but he loved riding in the car and Hazel had promised she wouldn't be long.

Rebecca hurried across the yard, her heart pounding with alarm. She was probably just imagining things; later she would feel like a fool....

She came to the door of the outhouse and peered inside, but it was too dark to see anything clearly. She groped for the light switch; but when she pressed it, nothing happened. Maybe the bulb had blown — but it had been working perfectly the evening before.

'Is there anyone there?' she asked, her eyes shining with dread, the sound of her own voice adding to her fears. The air was so still and close that the tension was almost palpable. Rebecca was tempted to turn and run, but something made her resist the impulse.

'Is there anyone there?' she asked again as she moved into the gloom of the shed. She tried to distinguish familiar shapes in the shadows — old implements that had once been used on the farm, bags of feed, nest-boxes for the hens. She lifted her eyes towards the rafters overhead; a few light cobwebs were draped about them here and there.

When she looked down again, her heart missed a beat. On the floor were a few bright-red splatters. Could it be blood? The thought made her quake.

The next moment she gasped in horror as she caught sight of the sheep's head glaring up at her.

Her thoughts raced, her nerves pulsated. Had some-one killed one of Hazel's sheep and cut its head off? No one could be so cruel....

The wool about the head was stained and matted with blood, and it made Rebecca's stomach churn even to look at it. Hazel was right: Maurice Warner was becoming more desperate. This was surely a warning that Hazel could expect more of the same if she didn't give in.

Rebecca knew she wouldn't be surprised if Luke was involved in this ugliness; he'd become very friendly with Maurice Warner and had been seen in his car more than once. But how could he have brought himself to kill one of the sheep out of sheer spite and malice? Or maybe the sheep's head had come from a butcher's yard or something....

Rebecca couldn't bear to look at the blood-smeared head any longer. But just as she turned away, the door was slammed shut and bolted from the outside.

'Let me out! Let me out!' she cried, pounding on the door with her hands; but she knew that no one would come to her until Hazel returned from the village.

She sank to the floor and sat on her haunches. Someone had been watching the house, seizing the moment when Hazel drove off, perhaps thinking that Rebecca was with her. It was a thought that made her shiver.

She glanced in vain at her watch — it was too dark to see it clearly. She was trying to distract herself, trying not to think of the ugliness in the shadows.

The minutes dragged by, but at last she heard Hazel drive up the hill.

'Let me out! Let me out!' she called again, when the car came to a stop, and Hazel rushed across the yard to set her free.

'What happened to you?' Hazel asked, concern in her voice.

Rebecca made no reply; she just pointed to the sheep's head.

When Hazel emerged from the shed, Rebecca saw the horror in her eyes.

'Is it one of yours?' Rebecca asked.

'No — no, I don't think so,' Hazel replied. She was clearly shaken. A brick through the window was one thing, but this was something entirely different.

'Are you going to telephone the police?' Rebecca persisted.

'I don't think so,' Hazel told her. 'It would only mean more publicity, and that would be playing into Warner's hands.' She came closer to Rebecca and put her arm around her, the first time she'd ever done so.

'I'm sorry you had to see the mess in there. I bet you're wishing you'd never come to stay with me at all.'

'No, no, I'm not,' Rebecca assured her. 'I'm just worried something even nastier is going to happen.'

'I wish I could promise you it won't, but I can't,' Hazel admitted. 'You go on inside now, and try not to worry. Try to think of nice things like the horses. I'll be in soon, when I've cleaned up here.'

A few moments later, Laurence appeared on the scene. When Hazel told him the news, he gasped in disbelief.

'This shouldn't be happening to someone like you, Hazel. You deserve to be happy,' he said, with a conviction that took her by surprise.

They stood at the top of the incline and looked over the darkened fields. 'I know it shouldn't be happening, but I suppose no one has a claim to happiness,' Hazel replied.

'Well, they should have,' Laurence said. 'You've always tried to be everyone's guardian angel, that's your trouble; maybe it's time you let someone look after you.'

Hazel looked at him curiously, but made no reply.

'We've both known what it's like to feel hopeless and alone,' Laurence went on, his voice slow and deliberate, as if the words were not easy to say. 'We've been friends a very long time, but now I'd like us to be something more.'

Hazel started to interrupt, but Laurence hadn't finished. 'Just promise you'll think about it. That's all I'm asking.'

Two days later, Rebecca was sitting at the breakfast table when she heard a news report on Radio Kerry that startled her. Rumours were rife that Staunton's timber business in Dereenard was about to close, the report said. The firm had been facing tough competition in recent years from larger, high-technology rivals elsewhere. Staunton's still relied on the use of forestry horses; its closure would be the end of an era.

'I don't believe a word of it,' Hazel said, when she came in from the yard and Rebecca told her about it. 'Just the Warners' rumour machine working overtime again.'

'But why would they do something like that?' asked Rebecca.

'Oh, they're trying to give Sam's customers the idea that he mightn't be around much longer,' Hazel replied, 'and that they'd be better off taking their custom somewhere new.'

'I didn't think people could get away with stuff like that,' Rebecca said. She was more worried than ever.

'People like the Warners can get away with almost anything,' Hazel told her. 'Anyway, the question is: what are we going to do about it?'

She was putting away the eggs she'd collected from the nest-boxes, and she continued in silence for a few moments.

'We'll finish up our jobs around here, and then we'll drive over to Sam's,' she announced, with her usual decisiveness. Jack barked his approval, and Rebecca couldn't resist a smile. The prospect of a drive in the car always appealed to Jack.

After breakfast, Rebecca helped her aunt with the rest of the chores, and about an hour later they were driving towards the village.

'It's about time we took the offensive ourselves,

instead of always waiting for Warner to say or do
something first and then reacting to it,' Hazel said
firmly. 'It may be a contest between David and Goliath,
but David might still have a few tricks left up his sleeve.'

Sam was more than surprised to see Hazel when she
strode into his office.

'Sam, I've come to put some order into this place,'
she told him, looking about her at the stacks of files,
some of them years old, piled high against the walls.

'There's no need for that. I know where everything
is,' Sam assured her.

'You may know where everything is, but you're
about the only one who does, Sam,' Hazel countered.
'And don't say, "What about the sheep?" — the sheep
can look after themselves for a few days.'

She gave Rebecca instructions to start clearing out
an old, almost-empty filing cabinet that stood in a
corner. 'And then, when we've sorted everything out,
Sam, we're going to set about getting you some new
orders,' Hazel went on, in a tone which would tolerate
no contradiction. 'And just because you're still using
the horses doesn't mean we have to turn our backs on
technology entirely. While Rebecca and I are making
changes here, you can go to Killarney and hire or buy
yourself a computer.'

Sam looked at her with the same surprise as before.
'What would I want with a computer, Hazel? Sure, I
wouldn't know the first thing about it.'

'Well, I would — or are you forgetting I took that
computer course in the evenings two years ago? Now,
off with you, and don't come back without some sort of
computer,' Hazel told him.

'Seems like I'm overruled, Jack,' Sam said, looking
at the sheepdog. 'So why don't you and I do as we're
told and go for a spin to Killarney?'

Jack barked with sudden enthusiasm. 'That dog would live and die driving around in cars,' Hazel said, and Rebecca laughed.

When Sam and Jack had left, Hazel glanced about the office again.

'You know, there were times when I thought Matt was a bit of a grumbler; nothing seemed to please him,' she said. 'But the more I think about it, the more I begin to see he might've had good reason to grumble.'

Hazel spent much of the day reorganising Sam's office, with Rebecca helping out as best she could.

'At least now all the old stuff's stored away in boxes and the new stuff's in some order in the cabinet, so if Sam says he can't find a thing any more, I'll kill him,' Hazel said.

Rebecca glanced now and then at receipts for payments to blacksmiths and saddlers and harness-makers, some of them years old. She wondered why Sam had kept them all, but in one way she was glad he had. They might have added to the clutter, but they proved — if proof was needed — what a vital part the forestry horses had played in the company, down through the years.

It was some time before Sam returned with the computer, and he watched with some bemusement as Hazel set it up. The office had been transformed; it looked much bigger and more spacious.

'It'll take me some time to get all your records, the recent stuff, onto this,' Hazel said, 'but when I do, you'll be able to call them up at the touch of a button, instead of having to spend half the morning searching through mounds of paper.'

'I liked my little searches, Hazel,' Sam said good-humouredly, 'and I'll be surprised if I ever get the hang of this yoke.'

'You will, Sam, you will,' Hazel promised. 'And when the records are sorted, I'm going to print up a new fact sheet about the company, with prices and stuff, and we'll send it out to see if we can generate some new business.'

'A lot of people are becoming more interested in the environment these days,' Rebecca said. 'Maybe some of them would be willing to support you if they knew they were supporting the horses too.'

'Most of my customers already know about the horses,' Sam said.

'Yes, your customers know about them,' Hazel agreed, 'but we're talking about new people here. Rebecca's right. Instead of thinking of the horses as some kind of weak link, maybe we should be using them as our strongest selling point. And do you know something, Sam? You haven't even got a horse in your logo.'

Sam was about to say he'd never thought very much about logos, but Hazel turned to Rebecca. 'Do you think you could come up with something this evening, Rebecca?' she asked. 'I know you wouldn't have much time, but we could use it at the top of the fact sheet.'

'I'd love to give it a try, if you think it's a good idea, Sam,' Rebecca said enthusiastically.

'Oh, anything Hazel says is fine by me,' Sam assured her. 'We're the only company in Kerry still using horses, so at least we're different — and we should highlight that difference.'

He started to make some coffee for his troops, as he called them. 'I only hope all your hard work will pay off in the long run,' he added, introducing a note of caution. 'I don't have to tell you, Hazel, it's dog eat dog out there in the real world.'

'Well, if it is, we'll eat dog with the best of them,'

Hazel said. Jack began to whine.

Rebecca spent much of the evening working on the new logo. Hazel had suggested something simple, and yet she found herself tearing out page after page.

'I thought I was fairly good at drawing horses, but I just can't get it right,' she told Jack, who was sitting beside her. It was as if he sensed she was doing something that was very important to her.

Hazel had the right idea, Rebecca thought: it was better to try and do something than to sit around and wait for things to happen. But were they building up their hopes only to have them dashed again? What if the letters they sent out produced no response? Worse still, what if Warners retaliated in some still more devastating way?

Rebecca was deep in thought, and Jack looked at her curiously, wondering why she made no movement with the pencil.

'Wouldn't it be awful if the summer I came to Dereenard was the same summer the forestry horses came to the end of the line?' she said aloud.

But in a moment she returned to her sketch. It was a very long time before she was satisfied with her work. The finished logo simply showed a horse, with the outline of a larch tree in the background, all enclosed in an oval-shaped cameo.

'It's very, very good!' Hazel told Rebecca. 'And I know Sam will like it too. Who knows? This little logo could be a symbol of a new beginning for him and the horses.'

'I hope it will be,' Rebecca said.

But, she thought, what if the future held an ending rather than a beginning?

Chapter Ten

*T*he news that Sam had received some new orders grated on Luke. He'd been waiting for the day when Maurice Warner would be in charge and the horses would be sent off to the knacker's yard, but now it seemed as if that day was further away than he'd imagined.

What Hazel could do with the office, Sam thought, he himself could do with the timber yard. That was why, one day, he asked the forestry workers to lend a hand, not just to clean and tidy and put things in order, but to do some painting too. 'This place has been looking a bit neglected this past while; it's about time we put things right,' he said with a smile.

Hazel was still busy in the office, putting the final touches to her new accounts system, which would help to simplify the process for the future, she promised. Rebecca, however, had decided to stay at home with

Jack; she would probably bring him down to the lake for a swim later in the afternoon.

Luke rubbed his stubbled chin with his hand. All the forestry workers down in the timber yard in the village — the perfect day to put a little plan of his own into action....

Some time later, a passerby on the road might have seen a figure hurry through the fields towards the forestry, its movements furtive and stealthy. The weather had been hot and sunny for the past few weeks, and the undergrowth was like tinder. A little sprinkling of petrol here and there, and one strike of a match — that was all it would take to put Sam and his cronies in their place once and for all. Luke's green eyes shone with vengefulness.

He hurried awkwardly down one of the forestry tracks, his heart pounding. No one would be able to point the finger of blame at him; a careless day-tripper and the remnant of a lighted cigarette was all it took to start a fire. He moved deeper and deeper into the wood, hoping desperately that no one had seen him. He carried a can of petrol in a carrier bag.

Leaving the sheep's head had been Maurice Warner's idea. But Hazel was not a woman who was easily frightened; if anything, it seemed to have spurred her into action again. A fire was a much better idea, much more practical; it could do so much more damage in the long run.

Luke chose a spot and began to gather together some rotten twigs and branches, still struggling to catch his breath after his dash along the path. He knew what they thought of him — just a nobody — but he would give them something to remember for the rest of their lives. People would talk about it for years to come — the day of the fire....

Every second was vital. He removed the can from the bag, fumbled with the cap and splashed the petrol around liberally. He smiled with anticipation as he took the box of matches from his pocket and prepared to strike one.

What he didn't know was that Sam had agreed that Laurence could remain at work at the forestry. Rafferty was growing stronger every day, and Laurence was anxious that he should get back to his old routine as soon as possible.

Just as Luke was about to strike the match, Laurence came running towards him.

'What are you doing here?' Laurence challenged. Luke started.

Laurence caught the smell of the petrol at once.

'I should've known you'd stoop to something like this,' he said angrily. 'But you're not going to get away with it.'

'And who says I'm not?' Luke demanded. 'You and Sam, you've tried to trample me into the ground long enough.'

He prepared to strike the match a second time, and Laurence took a step closer to him.

'Stand back! Stand back, I say!' Luke warned, bristling with resentment.

Laurence lunged at him, and they grappled with each other. Laurence was strong and muscular, but Luke gripped him with an unexpected fierceness.

'This is your style, Laurence, isn't it? Playing the hero,' he jeered.

'And what's your style, Luke? Running around like a sneak and hatching plots against your neighbours?'

Luke grabbed his opponent by the neck and squeezed, a kind of twisted pleasure in his eyes. Laurence tried to wrench the stubby fingers free, but it was as if Luke had the strength of madness in him. Laurence coughed and spluttered and gasped for breath, but Luke was relentless.

Laurence jerked his knee, struck his opponent in the stomach and sent him sprawling backwards. In an instant he was on top of Luke, struggling to pin him to the ground.

But Luke wasn't about to give up so easily. He struck a searing blow at Laurence's chest, dislodging him. They clung to each other more desperately still as they rolled around on the ground. They tore and clawed at each other, trying to get the upper hand; but it seemed to be a contest of equals. Would the loser simply be the one who was overcome by exhaustion?

Luke was driven by a thirst for revenge and a strange kind of injured pride; Laurence was motivated by a desire to protect the trees and the horses at all costs. Not only were the trees his livelihood; they also had a quiet beauty that could never be replaced. And the horses — the horses were his best friends.

Beads of sweat glistened on their foreheads; their clothes smelled of peat and leaves and oil. Laurence struggled on top of Luke, striving to hold him down.

'Sam was good to you, Luke,' he gasped. 'He gave you a chance when a lot of other people turned their backs on you. And this is how you repay him.'

'Why don't you pound me unconscious?' Luke jeered, unable to move. 'You know it's what I'd do if the shoe was on the other foot.'

'We aren't all like you, Luke. Some of us have minds of our own,' Laurence snapped. 'I'm taking you straight down to Sam in the village. He can decide what he wants to do with you.'

'And of course you'll be the big man again; you'll have saved the day!' Luke retorted mockingly.

He was groping over the ground with his right
hand, and at last his fingers made contact with a stout
branch. He gripped it tightly and, raising it high,
brought it down on his opponent's head.

Laurence moaned and fell backwards, and Luke
struggled to his feet in an instant. 'I told you you
wouldn't get the better of me this time, bucko,' he
gasped.

He took hold of Laurence's motionless body and
began to drag him along the ground. His heart
pounded with feverish intensity, and he looked about
him again and again. Laurence's boots left tracks in the
peaty soil, but Luke was too tense to worry about that.

At last he found a hollow and pushed Laurence into
it. He smiled with grim satisfaction. This was working
out better than he'd planned. He wouldn't have to rely
on some innocent day-tripper to take the blame for the
fire, after all; Laurence could be his scapegoat.

He ran back to the place where he'd gathered the
brushwood and scattered the oil, his entire being seized
with a kind of strange elation. He found the box of
matches again, struck a match and flung it from him.
The brushwood burst into flame, and the fire began to
spread.

'This will give old Sam something to think about,'
Luke said grimly. 'This will teach him to treat yours
truly like dirt.'

He was about to turn and run when something made
him think of the horses. He grabbed the petrol can
again and headed towards them. Here was a chance to
kill two birds with one stone: even if the other workers
were down in the timber yard, Laurence would still
have made it his business to harness both Rafferty and
Star. That was what he always did when his cousin
couldn't be at work for one reason or another; the two

horses were friends and they worked well together, he said.

Luke found Rafferty waiting patiently for his next load. His green eyes shone bright again.

'Oh, Sam would never get rid of the horses! No, Sam's too good for that. But there's more than one way to skin a cat,' he thought. He found a length of rope, tied it to the mouthpiece of the horse's bridle and lashed it tightly to the trunk of a tree. Rafferty shuffled restlessly.

'There, that should do the trick nicely,' Luke gasped. He ran off in search of Star.

It was only a matter of moments before he found him, crunching oats from a bag that Laurence had hung about his neck. 'You've had it too good for too long, my man,' Luke said, grabbing the bag and tossing it aside.

He tied Star to a nearby tree, just as he had tied Rafferty. He smirked and patted him on the neck; the horse recoiled at his touch.

'I see you've a long memory, you and Sam alike,' Luke jeered. 'But this is the end of the line, for you and for him.'

He unscrewed the cap of the can and scattered what was left of the petrol midway between the two horses. Seconds later, the brushwood burst into flame. Luke retreated at once, awkwardly retracing his steps along the pathway.

He hesitated and looked about him, debating what to do next. It made sense to leave the scene of the crime at once; but he was seized with a longing to savour the moment to the full. He hesitated another moment, then found a safe haven from which to watch the drama unfold.

The undergrowth was so dry that the fire raced

through it with frightening speed. The flames gathered round the trunks of the trees and set them alight, climbing higher and higher.

Rafferty and Star heard the furious crackling of the fire, and the ugly smell of burning filled them with terror. They grew more and more restless as the flames moved closer and closer to them. Rafferty struggled to break free, straining every muscle and sinew; but the rope held him firm, and the more he struggled, the tighter the knots became around the trunk of the tree. Clouds of smoke swirled about him, and he pawed the ground with his forelegs in an anguished frenzy.

Rebecca was playing games with Jack when she noticed the pall of smoke rising from the forestry. She looked at it with concern — but then, she thought, maybe it was nothing unusual; maybe Laurence had simply decided to gather up some dead brushwood and make a bonfire. Surely that would be foolhardy, though, when the place was so dry?

Jack saw the smoke too, and his agitated barking settled the matter for Rebecca. The two of them ran off through the fields towards the trees.

Rebecca hoped it really was just a bonfire lit by Laurence; but the more she thought about it, the less convinced she became.

'I hope nothing's happened to Laurence or the horses,' she said to Jack as they ran. Almost at once, she regretted putting her thoughts into words.

Jack reached the edge of the track before her, but he waited for her to catch up, his pink tongue hanging out. Rebecca was breathless, but a moment later she and Jack were dashing headlong down the path.

They hadn't travelled very far when they caught sight of the flames sweeping through the trees. The smoke was so dense that it pierced their eyes and throats and made them splutter.

'Maybe we should go and get help,' Rebecca said, her emotions a blend of horror and confusion. 'We can't do anything on our own.'

Next moment, however, she heard the whinnying of the horses. Jack's barking grew more furious still. It was as if he couldn't understand why she was dithering; they just had to rescue their friends.

On impulse, Rebecca tore a strip off her T-shirt and tied it about her mouth. She could hardly see a thing as she moved through the smoke; the flames were closing in around them on every side, their redness ugly and menacing.

'Be careful, Jack, be careful,' she urged as he led the way. But Jack's only thought was to save the horses.

Rebecca caught sight of the big chestnut horse, whinnying frenziedly. 'We're coming, Rafferty. We're coming!' she called out. But why was he tied to the tree? She didn't understand. Laurence never tied him.

She struggled to undo the knots. She discovered, to her horror, that they were as tight as they could be, and she wished she'd had the foresight to bring a penknife. She scraped and clawed at them with her fingernails, trying desperately to rip them apart, the whinnying of the horse and the barking of the dog ringing in her ears. The tough fibres of the rope cut at her flesh, making it raw and tender, but she persevered. Water streamed from her eyes, and she coughed and spluttered.

At last one of the knots came apart, then a second and a third. Whoever had started the fire must have tied the horses to the trees, Rebecca knew; but there

was no time to think about that now. And where was
Laurence?

She unwound the rope from the trunk of the tree,
then went to Rafferty to assure him he was free. 'Hurry,
Rafferty! Hurry!' she urged. 'There isn't much time.'

Rafferty, however, was disconcerted by the smoke
and the flames, and he refused to budge.

'Oh, Jack, can't you get him to walk on?' Rebecca
pleaded, her words muffled by the cloth about her
mouth. Jack barked encouragement to his friend, but
still Rafferty made no move.

'Stay with him, Jack, while I try and find Star,'
Rebecca told him.

A few moments later, she came upon Rafferty's
workmate. Again she struggled with the tight knots in
the rope. Star's movements were even more frantic and
unpredictable than Rafferty's; Rebecca saw the horror
in his wild dark eyes as he reared and neighed and
struggled to break free.

'Stand still, Star, stand still,' she begged desperately,
but his only response was to lash out with one of
his hind legs. Every second was vital; but the knots
stubbornly refused to give way. Rebecca tried to ignore
the pounding of her heart.

A tree came crashing down only a little distance
away, thudding against the ground, and she quaked
with fright. Star reared high again. There was no way
she was going to loosen the knots in time.

She pulled the sleeve of her T-shirt down over the
palm of her hand, then grabbed a burning splinter. Its
intense heat scorched her hand, but she held the flame
against the rope and the fibres began to burn.

It seemed like forever before the rope finally fell
apart, but in reality it was only a matter of moments.
Rebecca flung the splinter from her.

The coarse cloth bag that held the horse's feed caught her eye; somehow it had escaped the flames. She struggled to pull it over Star's head. He resisted vigorously, shaking his head this way and that, but at last she succeeded in putting the bag in place. 'It's better this way, Star,' she told him. 'It's better this way because you won't see the fire.'

She tugged at his bridle and tried to lead him forwards, but he resisted.

'Come on, come on — no one's going to hurt you now,' she cajoled, though her voice trembled. The raging brightness was all around them, and the smell of the smoke was suffocating.

A burning branch fell from its place, and Star reared high in fright, kicking wildly with his forelegs. Rebecca staggered backwards and fell to the ground; but in a moment she was lunging at his bridle again.

She stroked his neck. 'Come on, boy, please. You can trust me,' she pleaded.

At last he responded to the softness in her voice and followed where she led. Her movements were brisk and urgent, but she didn't run; she didn't want Star to panic again. She caught sight of a fox scurrying through the smoke. Like so many other animals, he was fleeing the fire.

She came to Rafferty and Jack. She adjusted the cloth about her mouth, then patted Rafferty and cajoled him again.

'Your friend's here now,' she told him reassuringly. 'There isn't any time to lose. We've got to get out of here.' She led the way with Star, hesitating to see if Rafferty would follow, and at last he did.

They had only taken a few steps when another tree came crashing down, right in their path. Star struggled to break free again. To Rebecca's joy and delight, however, Rafferty made his way round the fallen tree, its branches bright with fire; it was as if he were reassuring Star that everything would be all right.

Rebecca's admiration for Rafferty grew. Even though he could see the flames on every side, he had steeled himself against them and was taking the initiative again. 'Good boy, Rafferty, good boy!' she called to him.

Star was unable to see through the coarse cloth bag, but he sensed that Rafferty was forging ahead, and so he became quieter too. The smoke was growing denser, choking their breath. Rebecca could only hope that Rafferty knew the track so well that his instincts would lead them to safety. The soles of her shoes were scorched, adding the smell of burning rubber to the smoke. A bird fluttered overhead; she heard its restless flapping. The fire was out of control; nothing could stand in its way. All that mattered now was that they should reach the safety of the fields before it was too late.

Suddenly Rebecca's heart missed a beat: a hand had reached out and grabbed her.

Luke pushed her aside and blocked the path, brandishing a blazing branch in an effort to frighten the horses into bolting.

'There's no hope for you now, my beauties, no hope at all,' he jeered.

Rebecca flung herself upon him, pounding and kicking him with all the strength she could muster. She was acting on pure impulse; there was no time for rational thought.

Luke lashed out at her angrily. Jack joined in the fray, snarling at the end of one of Luke's trouser-legs.

'Clear off, you mutt — clear off!' Luke scowled; but Jack was resolute. The horses whinnied and turned away, but they were too afraid to move very far.

'Keep back, girl, keep back — or you'll get some of

this in the face,' Luke vowed, holding the lighted branch even closer to Rebecca.

Her only response was to kick him violently in the shin; he gasped and staggered, the branch slipping from his grasp. Jack pounced on him the moment he fell to the ground, growling more viciously still.

'I'll get you for this, you brute,' Luke snarled; but just as he was about to strike a deadly blow at the dog, Jack sank his teeth into his hand. Luke groaned with pain; blood spewed down the sleeve of his jacket.

Rebecca seized the moment to cajole the horses forward again. The fire still crackled and raged; but in a few moments, Rebecca saw a kind of brightness through the gloom. Her heart leapt with joy: the end of the track was in sight.

As soon as they had reached it, the horses galloped away from her, their sense of relief as palpable as her own. Jack came running towards her, and she patted him warmly.

But where was Laurence?

Rebecca didn't know it, but Laurence had roused himself from his stupor and had stumbled on Luke again. They grappled together. Laurence had never been more angry in his life, and his anger made him strong. One powerful blow and Luke slumped to the ground.

When Rebecca heard the movement on the pathway, she was seized with renewed terror; but then she saw Laurence dragging his rival to safety, and she sighed with relief.

She threw her arms about Laurence and hugged him close to her.

'It's over now,' he reassured her, 'all over now.'

The fire brigade was called, and, though a great deal of damage had been done, much of the forest was saved.

Luke was charged with arson; and Maurice Warner, fearing that he or his company might somehow be implicated in the bad deed, decided to abandon his plans for Dereenard. He had no problems with people doing unscrupulous things — as long as they had the good sense to get away with them, he reminded his brother the next time they spoke on the phone.

Rebecca felt very tired for a day or two, but the thought that the horses were safe filled her with delight, time and time again. Hazel was very proud of her; Rebecca might have been a bit reckless, but if she hadn't taken such decisive action, there was no telling what might have happened.

Sam was overjoyed. He was saddened that so many beautiful trees had been destroyed; but, thanks to Rebecca, the horses would continue to work at the forestry. And people had been very understanding — customers, too — all rallying round to offer what help they could.

'We're going to pull through, but we couldn't have done it without you two,' Sam told Hazel and Rebecca, when they came to see him in his office.

He had other news for them: he and Matt had patched up their differences. Matt had agreed to take over as Manager again, and Sam had promised not to be so critical in future.

'And the Coakleys can come back home!' Rebecca said happily. 'Warners have offered to sell them back their land.'

Sam smiled at her intensity. He had promised her a reward for all she had done, but the only reward Rebecca needed was the knowledge that the forestry horses would always be part of the scene in Dereenard.

One sunny morning, Rebecca and Jack went to visit Laurence and the horses in a part of the forestry untouched by the fire. Rebecca patted Rafferty, and was happy to see that he was back to his old self again.

'I don't know if I believe in fate or not, Rebecca, but I'm glad you decided to pay us a visit this summer,' Laurence smiled.

'I'm glad too,' Rebecca said.

'Change and change for the better aren't always one and the same, are they?' Laurence said. He came and patted Rafferty too, the light of the sun bright through the branches overhead.

Rebecca smiled. The forestry was a very special place, and she only had to see the power in Rafferty's shoulders, the brightness in his eyes, to know that he and his friends were very special too.

'You can give me a hand with planting the saplings in a little while, if you like,' Laurence suggested.

'Of course I will,' Rebecca promised. 'In a little while.'

Then she walked down the path with Rafferty and Jack, the placid chestnut horse drawing another log to the pile and the sheepdog barking with delight.

Also by Patrick O'Sullivan

Elsie and the Seal Boy

Some people say that the story of the baby abandoned at
Coonarone Bay and brought up by seals is only a legend.
But as Elsie is drawn into a mysterious water-world,
she discovers the wonderful truth....

Then greed for the *Ellen Maria*'s lost treasure threatens
the deep waters where the seal boy and the seals try to
live in peace. How can Elsie save her new friend's freedom?

A suspense-filled and magical tale of the bond
that can grow between humans and the wild.

ISBN 0-86327-558-3

A Girl and a Dolphin

What would it be like to see a real wild dolphin?
Anna finds out when an unexpected visitor
swims into her secret cove — a bottle-nosed dolphin!

As the summer slips by, their unusual friendship grows.
But the local fishermen don't want unwelcome guests
in their waters, and Donal's diving for sunken treasure
must remain undisturbed....

A story full of drama and adventure, which captures
all the magic of a wild creature living close to humans.

'A gripping tale.' *Irish Independent*

ISBN 0-86327-426-9

Available from
WOLFHOUND PRESS
68 Mountjoy Square, Dublin 1